Greg watched as Beth reached out and tucked an errant strand of hair behind his daughter's ear.

That simple gesture—so natural, so tender—drew him to her more than anything he'd seen her do or heard her say. Something about her instinct to nurture his daughter touched Greg deeply and roused emotions he had suppressed for months. For the rest of the evening he felt shy and uncertain around her, unable to meet her laughing eyes.

He told himself he was grateful when the evening ended early, and at the same time wondered why he was trying to think of a reason for Beth to stay….

Books by Anna Schmidt

Love Inspired

Caroline and the Preacher #72
A Mother for Amanda #109

ANNA SCHMIDT

has been writing most of her life. Her first "critical" success was a short poem she wrote for a Bible study class in fourth grade. Several years later she launched her career as a published author with a two-act play and several works of nonfiction. This is her tenth novel, and she hopes the second of many for Steeple Hill.

Anna is a transplanted Virginian, living now in Wisconsin. She works part-time doing public relations for an international company, and enjoys traveling, gardening, long walks in the city or country and antiquing. She is currently at work on a screenplay in addition to developing new story ideas for future novels.

A Mother
for Amanda
Anna Schmidt

❤️ *Love Inspired*®

Published by Steeple Hill Books™

STEEPLE HILL BOOKS

Steeple
Hill™

ISBN 0-373-87115-5

A MOTHER FOR AMANDA

Copyright © 2000 by Jo Horne Schmidt

Visit us at www.steeplehill.com

Printed in U.S.A.

For your faithful love is before my eyes
And I live my life by your truth.
—*Psalm* 26:3
The New Jerusalem Bible Translation

For all the dedicated souls who serve
as keepers of our glorious national parks.

Chapter One

Chief Ranger Greg Stone woke with a start, instantly on alert, his eyes wide-open as he lay in bed listening. Singing—bad and off-key—splintered the normal silence of the night. He glanced at his bedside clock. Two-twenty. In Yellowstone National Park only the nocturnal animals were usually stirring at this hour. No doubt one of the tourists from a nearby campsite had had a bit too much to drink and wandered into town.

Greg sighed as he sat up and reached for the pants to his uniform. The thing of it was that the singing was coming from a woman. Greg would have expected a male visitor to get drunk and make a scene but not a woman. Her singing was occasionally accompanied by a blast on a police whistle.

As he shoved his feet into well-worn but polished boots the shrill echo of her whistle pierced the night.

It was so loud it seemed to come from outside his own window. The woman was going to wake the entire town. Hastily he buttoned his shirt. Greg headed for the stairs, stopping only long enough to check on his ten-year-old daughter. Amanda was a solid sleeper, but this woman's ruckus could wake a hibernating bear.

Bear turned out to be the operative word. As Greg opened the door, he saw a large black bear circling a car parked just outside the unit next to his. Careful to make no sound, he observed the bear's actions from his position just inside his front door. The bear was trying desperately to get inside the car, pulling at the frame, clamoring over the hood, clawing at the windows. Greg frowned and released a grunt of exasperation. No doubt the owner of the car had left food inside, and the bear would use any means he could find to get at that feast.

"Stop that. Stop that right this minute," the woman demanded. "That car is brand-new, you dork. Who's going to pay for the damage you're doing?"

Greg rolled his eyes heavenward and retraced his path through his own house exiting by the back door. Once outside he eased around the corner to his truck and retrieved a stun gun from the cab. Knowing he was downwind of the bear, he worked his way to his half of the narrow front porch. As he stood in the shadows, he caught a closer glimpse of the woman.

She had ventured out onto the adjoining porch, and, in addition to her singing and whistle-blowing, she was madly waving her arms. From the noise she was making, he might have expected someone larger and more robust.

"Shoo," she ordered flinging her hands at the beast as if he were no more than a bothersome mosquito. Then she started to sing again. Her choice was "The Star Spangled Banner." The bear eyed her and returned to his work. In another minute he would succeed in prying open the passenger side door of the car.

"Just be very quiet and very still," Greg said softly and took particular pleasure in the gasp of surprise his voice elicited from her.

"Oh thank heavens," she gushed when she found her voice. "I have no idea what—"

"*Very* still and *very* quiet," he repeated as he moved into position. He raised the gun and aimed.

"Don't shoot," the woman shrieked just as the bear spotted Greg and paused in his dedication to ripping open the car. Greg fired and the bear dropped instantly and heavily to the ground. "Oh, my stars, you've killed him," the woman whimpered.

Greg put down the gun and headed for the bear. "I've stunned him, miss. He could have turned on you at any moment. Don't you know that you need to stay put if a bear is in the area? Waving your arms and making all that racket, you were taking a foolish and unnecessary risk."

"I thought I was *supposed* to make a lot of noise so he would know I was there," she reasoned.

Greg eased closer to the bear. "You're supposed to make sure there's no food in your car. You were just lucky that he was more intent on getting to the food. He's not going to be so lucky," he added ominously.

"What are you going to do?" Her eyes widened with fresh alarm.

Greg looked directly at her for the first time. It was a stretch to call the person on the porch adjoining his own half of the duplex a full-grown woman. She was barely a hundred pounds and certainly no more than an even five feet tall, but she carried herself with the kind of grace and ease of movement that could only have come from years of working out or participating in some other athletic endeavor. She had blond hair that fell in layers to the top of her shoulders and in the dim light her skin took on an almost translucent quality. Greg's detailed observation of her was the automatic response to years of practice in sizing up humans as well as animals for tips to possible behavior.

"We have to relocate him as far away from here as possible. We have to take him away from what he knows and understands and put him in a place where he'll have to settle in all over again," he lectured as he stood over the bear. "Read the rules, ma'am. If you're going to spend time here, you need to understand that you are the visitor here, not him." He nodded at the bear and scowled up at her.

"I guess I've managed to make quite an impression on my first night," she said softly as she glanced across the street. "So much for my hope to get here and get settled before introducing myself,'' she added with a smile.

Greg followed her gaze and saw lights on in the apartments where the seasonal help resided. It dawned on him that this dynamo responsible for rousting the entire community out of bed in the middle of the night was the new teacher from Chicago. He'd been hearing about her for weeks. Most of his information came from Amanda who eagerly reported every morsel of gossip she could gather about her new teacher. The book on her, according to Amanda, was that she was very young, very pretty and *very* rich.

Now that he thought of it, he recalled the park supervisor's assistant saying she was assigning the teacher to the vacant duplex. It had never occurred to him that the only vacant duplex was the unit next to his. He frowned and turned his attention back to the situation at hand.

"You should have secured the items in your car before going to bed," he instructed.

"I fell asleep. I meant to unpack, but I was so tired after the long drive," she explained, her eyes on the inert form of the bear. "He'll be all right?"

"He'll be fine—displaced but fine. Hopefully he won't find his way back here. If he does, next time we might not have any choice but to use a real bullet."

"No," she protested as if she actually thought she might have some say in the matter.

Greg glanced up at her. She might be the new teacher, but the fact was she looked too young to be

out of school herself and far too fragile to handle life
in a wilderness like Yellowstone. Compared to Evelyn Schuller, the woman she was replacing for the
year, she had to be a rookie—a rookie who was going
to attempt to teach in a place she obviously didn't
know the first thing about herself. "Look, Miss..."
He searched his brain for the name he'd heard the rest
of the staff talking about these past few weeks. All
he could remember was that she was the daughter of
some big industrialist back in Chicago.

"Beth," she replied, coming down one step of the
porch and offering her hand. "Beth Baxter."

Greg accepted the handshake.

"And you are..." she asked.

"Chief Ranger Stone," he replied. Normally he
didn't like throwing his title around, but in this case...

"So would I call you *Chief* or *Ranger?*" She
smiled a smile that reached her eyes. Greg looked
away. The woman was laughing at him. Her full
mouth was that close to breaking from a simple smile
into full-blown laughter.

"Greg Stone," he said keeping his tone formal and
stern. "About the bear, Miss Baxter..."

"Beth," she interrupted and moved in for a closer
look at the unconscious bear. "You probably saved
my car from total destruction, and I haven't even
thanked you."

There was that smile again. It seemed to come over
her all of a sudden as if she were incapable of con-
taining it. It lit her entire face, and he had to force

himself to look away. Never in his life had he seen a prettier face.

"I probably saved your life. Hopefully I'll be able to do the same for the bear," Greg said sternly. "Now if you'll excuse me, we have a great deal of work to do before he comes to." He headed across the street toward the administration building.

"You're just going to leave him here lying on my doorstep?"

Greg turned slowly and looked at her. "Beth," he began wearily. "That is a three-hundred-pound unconscious black bear. He brings new meaning to the term *deadweight*. I'm going to need some help loading him onto my truck and seeing that he gets to a safe place before he wakes up and realizes that whatever goodies you so thoughtlessly left in your car are still in there. With your permission, I am going across the street to the offices there and call the rangers on duty to give me a hand."

"Can I help?"

Most novices were cowed into submission by now in the face of his stern reprimand. This woman was impossible—she had that big-city arrogance. He'd seen it a thousand times in the tourists who annually traipsed through the park thinking they knew more than the rangers did. "Yes. Once we've removed the bear, you can unload the rest of the belongings from your car and get them inside. That done, hopefully—unless you are inclined to sing some more—you and the rest of the village can get at least a couple of hours of sleep." *There, he had resorted to insulting her out-right. That should do it.*

To his amazement, she laughed. "If it makes you feel any better," she called after him, "the bear didn't care all that much for my singing, either."

"I consider myself to be in good company then. Bears are notoriously discriminating in evaluating human traits," Greg replied and then he smiled to himself. He was very glad he had thrown out this last remark while walking away from her. He certainly did not want to leave the impression that he saw the situation as anything other than the dangerous foolhardy thing it had been.

Beth waited for him to return with two young rangers in tow and then sat on the step of the porch she shared with the unit next door and studied the human beast before her. Greg Stone was a take-charge kind of guy, but with an indefinable edge. She had the same sense about him that she had had about the encounter with the bear—she couldn't count on either of them to react according to the dictates of logic.

The chief ranger was tall and well-built. He certainly knew how to fill out that uniform. His close-cropped hair was the color of the bear's fur and his eyes were set deep beneath equally dark eyebrows. The eyes themselves were riveting, defying the object of his attention to look away. She watched in silent fascination as he and his two cohorts made quick work of moving and securing the bear in the back of a truck. There was no wasted action in his spare movements. In another place, another time, he might have been a dancer.

The other two rangers drove off into the night while the Chief Ranger stood watching them go. She sensed reluctance in him to turn around and face her, but he really had no choice. Unless he planned to stand there in the street all night, sooner or later he would have to acknowledge her again. She rested her elbow on one knee and her chin in her hand and waited.

"You can start unloading your car," he said as he walked briskly back toward the duplex. "I'll help."

"I can do it," she replied pushing herself to a standing position and stretching to ease the knots and cramped muscles she was experiencing after the long day of traveling. "You go ahead and try to catch some sleep. I expect you have to be on duty fairly early, especially at this time of the year."

He gave her a questioning look.

"I just mean that this must be the last few weeks of the high season in terms of tourists. I expect you have a lot to keep you busy these days." She could see that he was a little surprised at her observation. "Look, I know I made a big mistake and I'm sorry. I promise you that I have read the literature carefully. I just didn't expect I'd need to apply it within an hour of arriving here."

He made no reply but stood by the car waiting for her to open the trunk so he could begin unloading her things.

"You know, it feels as if I have just begun a grand

new adventure," she said amiably as she opened the hatch, "and frankly in spite of tonight's *mis*adventure, I must admit that I'm quite excited about the year here in Mammoth Hot Springs."

No response.

"I mean, who would have thought that a city girl born and bred who has lived her whole life in high-rise apartment buildings would find herself about to spend a year living and teaching in the wilds of Yellowstone National Park?"

He gathered a load from the car. Beth followed and because she always talked when she was nervous, she continued her monologue as if he had shown great interest in what she was saying.

"My friends and family think I am completely off my rocker," she continued and laughed as she stood for a moment surveying the quiet little town before her. "One thing is for certain—I am definitely out of my element." She laughed.

He didn't crack a smile. There were still a dozen or more boxes to go. Beth gritted her teeth and changed the subject determined to break the ice with this man who would be her neighbor.

"In Chicago, my days were filled with teaching duties at a very exclusive and expensive private school. My students were precocious and, far too often, they were also spoiled rotten." She tried to judge how this news was being received. His face was like untouched granite. "I'm really looking forward to meeting the children here," she added.

He looked at her, seemed about to comment, but then returned to the car for another load of boxes.

"I really love teaching," she told him, "but I was so sure that there was something more I could be doing—something I would never be able to experience in my safe little world there in Chicago. It was as if there was some connection I was missing. My life has been overscheduled for years between teaching and managing my responsibilities to my family. Did you ever feel that?"

"Not really," he replied stoically.

It was all the encouragement she needed to continue. "The day I saw the notice of the national exchange program, it was as if I'd been zapped by a sign straight from heaven. I mean, what were the chances that I'd be chosen for this assignment? It was like a burning bush or something equally dramatic— I love teaching and felt strongly that there was something more that I was supposed to be doing. Something was already telling me that I would never find the answers by staying in Chicago."

He looked at her with an expression of skepticism, but she ignored it. She was on a roll, talking as much for her own benefit as his as she tried to remind herself exactly why she had just driven straight through from Chicago to get here.

"The opportunity to come to Yellowstone was like a calling, and I feel certain that I am going to discover such new and important things here about the children, about myself and about life in general." She realized how self-serving that must sound to him.

"So, I packed up my stuff and here I am," she finished lamely.

"I'm afraid I don't believe in divine intervention, Beth. I believe in what I can see and witness right here on earth, and what happened earlier with the bear could have gotten nasty," he said clearly unconvinced that she grasped the seriousness of what had happened with the bear. "If you were counting on some higher power to intervene, you would have been sorely disappointed—and no doubt you would have ended up with a vehicle beyond repair."

She stared at him, trying to grasp the fact that he had finally responded to her in something other than monosyllables or cynical looks. One thing was certain, the man had a one-track mind and could clearly care less why she had come or how she was feeling about it.

"Thankfully none of that happened. You intervened—possibly at the instigation of that higher power—and I learned my lesson." She pulled a suitcase and a box tied with rope from the car and headed for the house. "I promise not to break any more rules, okay?"

"You have to respect the animals here. This is not Disneyland or Sea World," he warned as he watched her struggle with the heavy luggage. "You are on their turf here, not the other way around." He held up a bag of chocolate candy kisses she'd left on the passenger seat of the car. "If you leave something like this lying around, you're bound to have some unwelcome guests."

Beth set her burden down and sighed. She turned and faced the ranger who was a head taller than she was. "Yo, Chief Ranger Stone, message received and computed, okay? I screwed up. Judging from the number of lights that went on all around here, the entire staff is well aware of my faux pas. I get to be the newbie everybody can gossip about for the next couple of days. On top of that I get the distinct displeasure of explaining to my father just how I managed to let a bear destroy the paint job on a brand-new car. Punishment accepted. Now, drop it." She turned on her heel, picked up the luggage and attempted a purposeful stride into the house. She failed miserably, weaving from side to side due to her unbalanced load and the fact that she was bone weary.

Inside, she dropped the suitcase and box of books on the floor and turned to go get the next load. Greg Stone was right behind her carrying another large suitcase and two of the boxes. "Where do you want these?" he asked, his face as unreadable as a guard's outside Buckingham Palace.

"Anywhere, thanks." She brushed past him, caught a whiff of his freshly laundered and starched shirt and wondered if he slept in his uniform as she returned to the car for one last load.

"You brought a lot of stuff," he observed as he deposited the last of the boxes on the sofa in the crowded living room.

By now she was hearing every word from his mouth as a reprimand. "School supplies, teaching tools," she said through gritted teeth, wondering if he thought every box was filled with clothes. "Except for that one," she added as she relieved him of the last suitcase. She lowered her voice to a confidential tone, "In here I carry my sky-blue-pink chiffon ball-gown and the ruby-and-sapphire jewelry I always wear to church on Sundays. I've asked my designer, Pierre, and my hairdresser, Fifi, to join me here by the end of the week. The butler and upstairs maid I figured I could do without. I mean, what's the sense of roughing it if you don't make a few sacrifices, right?"

He looked so totally confused that she almost took pity on him, but she also saw in his half-believing expression that word of her family's wealth and social position had been part of the information that had been shared prior to her arrival. She hadn't even been here a day and already she had embarrassed herself in front of the whole staff as the novice and city slicker that she was. Suddenly she was exhausted and wondering if she had made the right decision in coming here after all. "Good night, Chief Ranger," she said wearily.

"Good night," he replied and she heard him open the screen door. "You know it was probably a really good idea to leave the butler and maid behind," he observed somberly. "On the other hand, I'm looking forward to church Sunday. I've never actually seen a color like sky-blue-pink before. Good night, Beth and welcome to Yellowstone."

Beth listened as he walked across the porch. She heard the squeak of the door of the unit next to hers.

She heard the sleepy voice of a child and the deep rumble of the ranger's reply. She stepped to the open door of her own unit and listened for another voice—a woman's voice, his wife's voice, but then he closed the door and all she heard was the silence of her first night in Yellowstone Park.

Beth stepped out onto the porch and took a deep breath as she let the silence and the scent of the night engulf her. The air was clear and cool for August, and she wrapped her arms around herself for warmth. She sniffed the odor of sulfur and knew the fumes came from the spectacular cascade of terraced springs for which the village was named. She looked forward to the day when she would barely notice the scent—it would mean that she had settled in and become a part of this place.

Maybe it *had* been a mistake coming here. Clearly Chief Ranger Stone would agree with that. She had left behind a career at one of the top private schools in the country. She had also left an active social life built mostly around her position as the only heir to the Baxter fortune, a family fortune that went back three generations. Her father, Thomas Baxter, was one of the most respected and popular businessmen in the Midwest. Her mother, Elizabeth, was a legend in the city for her grace and generosity.

Her parents would never stand in the way of her trying something new, but they had clearly had their doubts about this particular adventure. As he'd helped her pack her car, her father had said only one thing. "It's not too late to change your mind, honey."

"It's Yellowstone, Dad, not the ends of the earth, and besides it's only a nine-month assignment."

Her father had sighed and hugged her hard. "Lately, it just seems as if you're struggling to find your place in this world," he said. "That can be a time when a person might make decisions on the fly and regret them later. I just don't want you to think that you can't change your mind. You spend a month or so there and if it doesn't feel right, come on home, okay?"

She stared out at the quiet little town. She had not expected it to be quite so dark. It wasn't that she had expected streetlights like she knew back home in Chicago, but it was uncommonly dark—inky black to be more specific, like stepping into a great unknown, which was, of course, exactly the case.

It occurred to her that perhaps the reason she had left Chicago was to find a place of her own—a place not first connected to her family's name and history. She was proud of her family and all that they had accomplished, but she had a need to be her own person—to prove to herself that she was strong and capable in her own right.

She listened and heard silence—no cars, no televisions blaring, nothing but the slight murmur of the evergreens rustled by the wind. Across the way, the lights in the other units had been turned out and people had hopefully gone back to sleep. She took another deep breath and closed her eyes, thanking God again for dropping this incredible opportunity in her lap.

She stepped off the porch and into the street. With her head thrown back and her eyes still closed, she spun slowly around. *"I won't let you down,"* she said softly. *"Thank you, God, for bringing me to this wonderful place and thank you in advance for guiding my footsteps in the days to come."* She opened her eyes and focused on one twinkling star that seemed to shine directly on her. It tickled her to consider the possibility that God was looking down and winking at her. Then she heard the cry of something she could only identify as wild and primitive and far too close for comfort. She quickly stepped back inside her unit and closed the door. She was pretty sure the primal cry in the black night was not God talking back to her, and she was even more certain that Chief Ranger Stone would not look kindly on having to rescue her twice in one night.

Chapter Two

In the bright light of morning, Beth surveyed her new home. It was clean, compact, utilitarian and *beige*—there were no other words to describe it. The walls were beige, the carpeting was beige and the well-used upholstered furniture was beige. Even the kitchen appliances were beige. Beth searched through the boxes until she found her grandmother's colorful crazy quilt. She tossed it over the sofa and stood back to admire the effect. That quilt had traveled with her to boarding school, summer camp and college. Its colorful collage of patches had withstood the roller coaster of emotions that were a part of any growing girl's life, and it looked right at home here in this new environment.

"Perfect," she murmured as she returned to the boxes for other items that would make this place *her* place. She longed to bang nails in the walls and hang comforting posters of pristine blue lakes and fields of wildflowers. She had passed a store on her way through town the night before. As she made a list of items she would need, she wished she had packed the crayon-colored dishes that stocked the open shelving in her kitchen back in Chicago. Perhaps she could offset the bland whiteness of the unit's dishes by quilting some colorful place mats. At least the dishes weren't beige. Shelf paper might brighten the cabinets a little, she thought and added that to her list.

She wandered back upstairs to the bedroom and immediately began rearranging the furniture into a less regimented, homier pattern. She spotted an old cane-seated rocker. It was the first thing she'd seen in the place that had a hint of character, and she decided it belonged in the living room. As she wrestled the chair down the stairs, she began to see potential for the place. Rustic, but not impossible.

"Yoo-hoo," a woman's voice called out a few hours later as Beth unpacked books and loaded them into the too small bookcase built into the end of her kitchen counter.

"Come in," Beth replied as she gave up trying to cram one more volume into the tiny space and stood to greet her visitor.

"Hi, Beth, I'm Connie Spinner," a tall angular woman of about forty announced as she crossed the room extending her hand in welcome. "I teach the first graders and my husband, Al, is on the school board? Big galoot, kind of the *aw-shucks, ma'am* type?"

Beth smiled and wiped her hand on her jeans before accepting the welcoming handshake of the other woman. "Of course, I remember him. I try to remember anyone who gives me a job," she said.

Connie laughed. "Honey, you had the job on paper. Offering to come to Bozeman for an in-person interview just about blew everybody here away. The school board decided it would be downright rude not to meet you face-to-face if you were willing to go to all that trouble." She stepped back and surveyed the room. "Not much to look at, is it?"

"Oh, it has some real possibilities," Beth said with as much enthusiasm as she could muster after a morning spent scrubbing cabinets and trying to arrange the available furnishings into some semblance of a comfortable and welcoming living space.

"You're being way too kind and polite. The good news is that we might be able to supplement these ragtag furnishings a bit if you tell me what to look for." Connie spotted the piles of books. "Bookcases would be my guess for a start. You sure did bring a lot of reading material."

"Those are mostly materials and workbooks for the school. If the bookcase situation there is better than here, then I should be okay." Beth smiled. "How about a cup of coffee?"

"A quick one. I have to get back to the store before the tourists overwhelm Al. He gets to gabbing and before you know it, people have either given up on ever getting checked out or they've walked out without paying. Either way we lose business and here at the end of the season every sale counts." She pulled a pad of paper and pencil closer as she perched on one of the two mismatched bar stools next to the counter. "So, at least one more bookcase. What else?"

"A floor lamp for next to the rocker there?" Beth didn't want to push her luck but...

"Floor lamp. How about for the bedroom? Have you got lighting up there because those ceiling things will blind you for sure if you're planning to read in bed."

Beth smiled. "I wouldn't turn down a nice bedside light," she admitted.

Connie wrote it down. "What else?"

Might as well address the subject up front, Beth decided. "How about a nice bear deterrent?" she said.

Connie looked startled and then gave a hoot of laughter. "Oh honey, don't you worry about that. There isn't a person in this place that couldn't have just as embarrassing a story told on them—including Greg Stone."

"I can't imagine him ever not doing things by the book and being as perfect as his freshly pressed and starched uniform," Beth said.

"Greg Stone? By the book? The man has broken more rules in his day than any of us. He was born and raised in the park system, knows just about every inch of this place and sometimes it goes to his head a bit. He can be something of a rebel, but he knows his stuff."

"Well, he certainly wasn't cutting me any slack last night."

Connie frowned. "He's changed some. Goes back about a year and a half. His wife died—cancer. He'd just been made Chief Ranger when she got the diagnosis. I think Greg grew up real fast that day. I expect we all looked at life a little different after Lu died." She sat for a long moment staring at the notepad in front of her.

Beth's heart went out to the woman who had clearly lost a good friend. She also thought about Greg Stone and remembered the child's voice from the night before. She handed Connie a mug of steaming coffee. "I'm so sorry for your loss," Beth said softly.

Immediately Connie brightened. "Thanks, but the fact is that it's true what they say about time healing all wounds. Lu certainly wouldn't want people sitting around remembering her with mournful faces. 'Live life or lose it,' she used to say even before she got sick. It's sound advice. "

"Has time healed all wounds for Greg?" The words were out before Beth could stop them. She blushed. "I'm sorry," she hastened to add. "This really is none of my business."

"Honey, in a community as small as this one is, you'll soon learn that everything is everybody's business," Connie assured her. "It's only natural that you'd wonder. After all, Greg's daughter, Amanda will be one of your students." She paused for a minute as if casting about for the right words. "Greg is...

Time may not have been as kind to Greg as it has been to the rest of us.''

"And his daughter?"

Connie grinned. "Amanda is a treasure. Sometimes I think she took the whole thing better than us grown-ups. Lu did some good work helping Amanda prepare for the end and all.'' She reached across the counter for the sugar bowl and dumped three teaspoons of sugar into her coffee and stirred it briskly. "Have you been over to the school yet?"

"I thought I'd get things settled here first and then go over and start setting up things for next week's opening day,'' Beth replied glad to be off the subject of the tragic loss of the ranger's wife.

"Come on. Let's go ahead and get some of these supplies over there now. You may as well get the lay of the land right away. I'll walk you over to the school. I want to check on something in my classroom on my way back to the store. Besides, there's not much more you can do here anyway, right?'' Connie picked up one of the boxes plus her coffee and headed for the door leaving Beth no alternative but to do the same.

Just outside the school, Connie spotted Greg. "Hey, Stone, come on over here and give us a hand,'' she called as she and Beth juggled the boxes of books.

Beth watched the ranger's approach. Was it her imagination that he proceeded toward them with some reluctance? Reading his expression was impossible since his features were hidden in shadow thanks to the wide brim of his hat.

"Connie. Beth," Greg said politely as he took the large box Connie was carrying and then turned to Beth. "You can put that one right on top," he instructed.

"As long as you've got everything under control, Greg, I'll leave Beth in your capable hands and run on ahead. I just want to check to be sure they finished painting in my room and then I've got to get back to the store." Connie turned her attention to Beth. "Now you stop by the store later and say hello to Al, okay? Meanwhile I'll see what I can drum up in the way of furnishings for that place of yours."

"Thanks, Connie. Thanks for stopping by." Beth was actually reluctant to let the woman go since it meant she would be alone with Greg. Clearly he had not revised his opinion of her much from the previous evening's encounter. On top of that, he looked as fresh and starched as usual while she'd been unpacking all morning and felt dirty and in need of a good shower. She brushed back her hair and tucked the tail of her T-shirt into her jeans.

"Could you get the door?" Greg said politely after they had followed Connie inside and gone past her room to a room at the end of the hallway.

"Oh, sure. Sorry." Beth rushed to open the door for him. "Just put them down anywhere. They must weigh a ton. I could barely manage one of them and…oh my…"

Beth walked slowly around the sixth-grade classroom, trailing her fingers over the worn polished desks, studying the displays on the bulletin boards and taking note of not just one, but three, computers in the corner of the room. "I can see I'm going to have some major shoes to fill," she said softly. "Clearly Evelyn Schuller loves teaching as much as I do."

"Evie Schuller was born to teach," Greg replied as he sat the heavy boxes down with a thud. "She regularly goes after the Washington bigwigs to get the latest equipment for these kids. She's determined that they won't be behind when they leave here and head for the mainstream school up in Gardiner."

"Well, I'll just have to do whatever it takes to live up to her standards," Beth stated.

"Evie was certainly in favor of your selection," Greg said and she could feel him studying her as if he didn't quite understand why *anyone* much less the revered teacher would think Beth could do the job. "Not that there were that many other applicants. Not too many people are anxious to spend a winter in Yellowstone if they know anything at all about how isolated and shut down things can get."

Beth understood that there was an unasked question there somewhere. She waited.

"Do you have any idea what you've let yourself in for, Miss? It can get pretty lonesome here once the tourists leave and things shut down. There's no night-life, no excitement to speak of."

Beth sighed. So, here it was again, the assumption that coming from the city she must be used to life in the fast lane. "Well, of course, I can't know for sure since I've never lived through a winter here, but I think I'll be okay," Beth said and she knew she sounded a little defensive.

"Why would you leave what was surely a comfortable life in Chicago?" Beth guessed that Greg was asking a question that had been the topic of discussion among other park employees. "I mean, the city must be a pretty exciting place to live," he continued considering each word. "I would imagine you might miss that. On the other hand, I've seen people come here because they're running from something." He pinned her with his gaze.

"I'm not running away from anything," Beth assured him and then decided she might as well test the waters. "Do you believe in God, Ranger Stone?"

Greg locked his hands behind his back and walked the length of the classroom as if on patrol. He glanced at the colorful bulletin boards and then settled on staring at the view from the windows. "It's been said that you could bring the biggest atheist in the world here to this place and inside a week, that person would be a full believer."

"That wasn't the question," Beth replied. When he said nothing, she continued. "As I mentioned last night, I think that God brought me here. I'm not sure why yet, especially now that I've seen Evelyn's classroom. I thought it was to make some difference for the children, but now I have to think it might be something else."

He remained silent as if waiting for her to continue, so she did.

"Back home in Chicago, I felt this…restlessness—

for lack of a better word. With my work, myself, my life in general. That's when I saw the announcement of the exchange program. It seemed to be just the right solution.''

Greg scowled at her. "I hope you aren't about to tell me that you've come here out of some misguided intent to *find yourself.*"

"No. That's not what I—"

"The children will need your complete attention," he said sternly interrupting her before she could explain.

"Of course. I just meant that—"

"Beth, please believe me when I tell you that I fully appreciate the romanticism that is often attached to Yellowstone. There is a powerful mix of ingredients at work here—incredible scenery, awesome power of nature, the last real frontier in a country that has based its entire history on conquering new frontiers. All of it can add up to expectations that may be unrealistic. For a tourist—here for a few days or a week—there's no harm in the fantasy. For someone who will reside here for a number of months and have responsibilities that affect the lives of our children, such fantasies can be dangerous."

Beth stared openmouthed at the tall ranger. She thought about what Connie had told her about how much he had changed since the death of his wife. She tried to convince herself that somewhere under all that starched rigidity was a living, breathing, feeling human being who was not immune to the power of a moment. She tried to tell herself that in time she would prove to him that she was every bit as qualified as the woman she was replacing for the year.

"If there's nothing else you need moved, Beth, I'll be going," he said and headed briskly up the center aisle toward the door.

"Ranger Stone," she called after him. He paused but did not turn back to face her. "Just so that we are clear about one thing here—I am an experienced and respected teacher. I am very good at what I do, just as I'm sure you are. In my business, a little imagination goes a long way toward making for a successful day. I'm sorry if your work in these glorious surroundings no longer seems to afford you the same opportunity."

Without another word, he left the building. Beth stood at the window of her classroom and watched him stride across the compound. As he walked away without a backward glance, she felt the tiniest suspicion that there might be an element of truth in what he said. Other than Connie, Greg Stone was the only other person she'd met here. She had deliberately left behind everyone and everything she cherished to spend this year in a place where she knew no one and where the surroundings and life-style were a far cry from anything that even remotely resembled what had passed for normal in her life so far. The whole idea was definitely more daunting in the light of day than it had been the night before.

That afternoon, Beth decided she'd better do something about her car. She drove back to Gardiner, the small community closest to the northwest entrance to the park, hoping to find a dealership or at least a qualified shop to repair the damage the bear had done to her car.

When she had called her parents to tell them of her safe arrival, she had skimmed over the extent of the damage and had definitely left off the part about the scratches being caused by a bear. She drove through town twice before settling on a service shop near the edge of town.

"Hi," she said to the pair of scuffed cowboy boots protruding from under an ancient pickup truck. "Can you help me?"

A woman of about fifty rolled herself out from under the truck and squinted up at Beth as she wiped her hands on a grease-covered rag. "That all depends," she said.

Beth waited. The woman waited.

"On what?" Beth asked politely.

"On what you need help doing," the woman replied.

"My car has some paint damage. Do you handle that sort of thing?"

"Paint damage? Let me take a look." She got to her feet and walked out to where Beth had left the car parked near the garage door. "Left some bear bait inside, did you?" The woman didn't seem to expect an answer as she strolled slowly around the car. "More than one?" she asked.

"Pardon?"

"Bear. More than one bear?"

"No. Just one."

The woman clicked her tongue against her cheek and shook her head sadly. "Gonna need the full works," she muttered more to herself than to Beth. "You like green?"

"Green?" Beth was beginning to feel as if she'd walked into a foreign land where she clearly did not understand the language.

"I've only got green—dark like the evergreens. Nice."

"I see. You know, maybe if it's that big of a job I should go to Billings or Bozeman."

"Suit yourself," the woman replied and walked immediately back into the garage where she lay down on the dolly and slid back underneath the pickup.

"Can I use your phone?" Beth asked. "I'll charge the calls to my calling card."

"Suit yourself," the woman repeated.

Beth turned and walked smack into the chest of Chief Ranger Stone. It was turning out to be a delightful day.

"Problem, Beth?"

"Nothing I can't handle," she replied primly.

"Stone? Is that you?" The dolly rattled out from under the truck and the woman smiled broadly as she leapt nimbly to her feet and pumped Greg's hand.

The man actually smiled. "Hello, Gracie. How have you been?"

"Been missing you, you big long drink of water. It's about time you stopped by." She punched him hard in the arm and cackled with delight. "Did you hear about this one here?'' She waved a hand in Beth's general direction. ''Got her car tangled up with a bear. Look at the mess he made of that paint job. Looks like a brand-new car, don't it? Pity.''

''Can you help her?'' Greg asked.

''She don't want green. Green's all I got in stock.''

''I see.'' Greg and the woman called Gracie continued to consider Beth's car as if she had suddenly become invisible. ''What's wrong with green?'' he asked and Beth realized the question was aimed at her.

''Nothing. It's just that—''

''She's not from around here, Greg. If she thinks she can do better up in Bozeman or Billings, that's no skin off my nose.''

''Gracie's the best there is,'' Greg told her.

''I'm sure she's very good but as you can see the car is red.''

''And?'' Greg waited.

''And…it's red,'' she repeated lamely.

''So, it will be green or it'll rust. Seems a pretty simple choice. Trust me, you do not have the time to go all the way to Bozeman two or three times and even if you did, how would you get back and forth while they've got your car?''

Beth had to admit that she had not considered that.

''Let me show you the color, sweetie,'' Gracie suggested kindly. ''I didn't know you was a friend of Greg's. We can order anything you want, but let me show you the green, okay?''

''Sure,'' Beth replied not wanting to appear rude.

"It's real nice," Gracie continued as she rummaged through an overstuffed desk. "Ah here. These are the color charts and I got this one."

It was a very nice shade of deep green. Beth studied the chart and the manufacturer's claims. "It is nice," she admitted.

"It's recommended for your make and model," Greg noted as he read over her shoulder. "When can you do it, Gracie?"

Gracie shrugged. "Could have it finished for you by Tuesday week."

Greg and Gracie turned their attention to Beth.

"If you like, you can leave it now and ride back with me," Greg offered in that stiff formal way he had of speaking to her.

"How much?" Beth asked, clinging to her last hope for refusing.

Gracie did some figuring with a stubby pencil on a grease-smeared and torn piece of paper and handed it to Beth.

Beth could not believe the figure. "How much for your labor?" she asked.

"I figured that in," Gracie replied and waited.

It was a ridiculously low figure. "Is there a guarantee on the workmanship?" she asked, knowing she was being impolite but they were talking about a car worth about what she would be paid in salary for the year.

Greg cleared his throat. "I will personally guarantee the work," he said. "If for any reason it does not meet your satisfaction, I will pay to have the car repainted somewhere else.''

"Bless you, son,'' Gracie murmured.

Beth saw no way out. "Green it is,'' she said and turned to take a last look at her beautiful red car.

Gracie grinned. "You won't be the least bit sorry, darling. I'll just need the key.''

Beth worked it off the ring and handed it to the mechanic.

"See you soon, Gracie,'' Greg said as he leaned down and kissed the woman on the cheek. "Ready?'' he said in Beth's general direction as he headed back toward his truck.

"See you Tuesday week,'' Gracie called.

"Don't you need a downpayment?'' Beth asked reaching for her purse.

"Heck no, sweetie. I know where you hang out, and I got Greg there to track you down if you try to skip town.'' Gracie walked Beth to the passenger side of the truck as if they were old friends. She opened the door for her. "You be good to this little lady, Greg Stone.''

Greg tipped his hat. "Yes ma'am,'' he replied and shifted into gear. "Just thought you'd like to know that it's a pretty good hike from here to Mammoth,'' he said as they headed down the highway. "I'm sure you had it all worked out how you were going to get back in time for school to start next week, but it would have been quite a hike since there's no car rental place in Gardiner.''

Beth slumped farther down in the seat. The one

thing she had always hated more than anything was appearing stupid. She now amended that to be that the one thing she hated more than anything was appearing stupid in front of Greg Stone.

He drove in blessed silence for several miles giving Beth the time she needed to compose herself and begin to take an interest in the sights around her.

"I see some gold but no reds or coppers in the turning of the leaves. Do they come later?" she asked.

"Autumn color west of the Mississippi tends to be a little less splashy. The gold on those quaking aspen there pretty much has to make up for the lack of other fall colors," Greg replied.

Beth saw that he was more comfortable with conversation about the park and certainly it would make the trip go faster if they talked about something.

"They are beautiful," she agreed. "Those white trunks against the deep green of the evergreens, and just look at the way the leaves shimmer and rustle with just the slightest breeze." She laughed. "Thus, the name *quaking*, I suppose."

They left the aspen behind and entered a forest of very tall, very skinny evergreens.

"Lodgepole pines," Greg explained before she had a chance to ask. "They grow to be about one-hundred feet tall and stay pretty thin in diameter. They cover most of the forested areas of the park."

"They are so tall and elegant in their thin stately beauty," she said. "Some of their trunks are blackened. Have they been burned?"

"Scorched in the fires of '88 but these made it.

Other places there are whole stands that were completely destroyed. It's one of the things you're likely to see as you travel the park. A couple of recent isolated fires have left some forests pretty much ghosts of what they were. The trees are still standing—the trunks are, but it's important to remember that they are deceptively sturdy and secure. Beneath the soil of the burned out trees there is no root system to hold them.''

''That's so sad.''

''Not really. Fire is a natural thing in a wilderness.''

''Fascinating.'' She settled back and watched a flock of Canada geese fly overhead. They were no doubt on their way to the Yellowstone River. In the meadows were herds of bison grazing and in the distance she saw pronghorn antelope frolicking in the field.

''This must have been what it was like when the settlers headed west,'' she murmured more to herself than to him. ''These are the sights they saw. It's absolutely awesome.'' Her voice shook with emotion.

Greg glanced over at her. His hat was on the floor between them and the wind ruffled his dark hair. She was aware of his deeply tanned hands on the steering wheel—strong hands that might have belonged to such a pioneer and it struck her that in his own way, Greg Stone was a frontiersman.

Confused by the emotions she felt, she focused her attention back out the window. ''Oh, look, that elk herd is twice as large as the one in town. They are magnificent. Look at the way the male stands there keeping watch.''

Greg pulled into an overlook and shifted into neutral. ''That's his harem. He's making sure some other bull doesn't come along to challenge him for his women.''

''Really?'' Beth was fascinated at this piece of information.

''It's the rutting season for many of the species. The males stake their claim on the females and defy any other male to come along and challenge that claim. That's what all the bugling you've been hearing in town is about.''

Beth felt a growing respect for the ranger. ''Tell me about your job. What exactly does a chief ranger do?''

He actually laughed. ''Rangers at all levels wear a variety of hats. We are the police, firefighters, animal handlers, naturalists, cowboys and medics. For the human animal we also have to sometimes play the role of parent, guide and psychologist.''

''You mean for the visitors to the park.''

''There are visitors and there are tourists,'' he said with a touch of regret. ''Unfortunately, we mostly get tourists.''

''What's the difference?''

''For tourists the average stay in the park is a day and half. You can't really do much except hit the highlights in that short of a time.''

''And visitors?''

He looked straight ahead at the road as he pulled

out of the overlook. "Visitors stay longer, but they still leave eventually."

"Like me?"

"Yes, ma'am."

Chapter Three

Several of the children had stopped by the school on the pretense of helping her set up for opening day. Beth understood that the children were driven by curiosity. Based on her one-sided conversation with the chief ranger the night she arrived, she had no such illusions about him.

"Mrs. Schuller always kept the reading books on that shelf," one of the girls instructed as Beth prepared to move them to a bookcase on the other side of the room.

"I don't think that Mrs. Schuller will mind if I change things around a bit," Beth replied. "Where do you think we should set up the science corner?"

The children were alternately shy with her and curious about what kind of year they could expect.

"Mrs. Schuller put it there," the same girl announced.

"I think that's perfect," Beth said and saw the girl smile.

Her students ranged in age from nine to eleven. Connie had warned her that the older children would not hesitate to be quite outspoken about how things were to be done. Beth was amused by the way that they made sure that their conversation was peppered with comments that began, "Mrs. Schuller always…" or "Mrs. Schuller used to…" She tried to encourage them to talk about how school had been before and what they might expect now that she was there. They were clearly coming from very different lives from the children she had taught in Chicago. Their comments gave her insight into their concerns and anxieties about how the year with her might go.

"Okay, I think we've made some real progress here today," she said. "Thank you, children, for stopping by to help. I couldn't have done it without you."

She glanced up and saw Greg Stone standing in the doorway to the classroom. "Everything all right here?" he asked in that serious gruff voice that seemed to be his signature.

"Fine," Beth replied. She wondered if the chief ranger was checking up on her. "Haven't seen a bear all morning," she added and saw the children's eyes widen in surprise.

Greg frowned. "Just checking."

Now that she knew about his wife's death, Beth could not deny that she was curious about the man. She was touched by his efforts to raise his daughter on his own. Her first instinct had been to find some way to be helpful especially since she was living right next door. She had considered and then rejected several ideas. She could invite them over, but that might seem too forward. She could host a party and include them, but other than the Spinners, she really didn't know anyone well enough to invite them for a party yet. It occurred to her that the other children had given her the perfect solution.

"Oh, Chief Ranger Stone," Beth called out as he turned to leave, "please tell Amanda that she's welcome to stop by any time. The other children have been quite a help to me, but they tell me that Amanda has some wonderful ideas as well. Isn't that right, children?"

Four heads nodded in unison as they turned from Beth to Ranger Stone as if they were watching a tennis match.

The ball is in your court, Beth thought and smiled.

"I'll let her know," he replied and hesitated.

"Was there something else?" Beth asked.

He glanced at the children. "No, that'll be all," he said and left the room. It did not escape Beth how he had dismissed her when he was the one leaving.

Over the next several days, Amanda continued to keep her distance although Beth had seen the child watching her comings and goings. Once when Beth smiled and waved, Amanda had pretended not to see her and concentrated all of her attention on straightening the curtains of the living room window on her half of the duplex. Connie had told Beth about

Amanda's close relationship with Evelyn Schuller, so Beth had decided to let the little girl come to her rather than trying to seek her out. She wondered if Greg had influenced his daughter's opinion of her new teacher. It was definitely clear that he had his doubts about Beth.

By the time Sunday came, Beth had actually grown used to the sight of elk grazing in her front yard and buffalo—or bison, as the locals preferred—wandering across the road. She had also met several other human residents from the village. Everyone was polite, but it was clear to Beth that at least some of the others shared Greg Stone's reservations about her.

"Good morning, Beth," Connie called out as Beth approached the park's chapel. As usual the gregarious woman drew Beth into the circle of park employees standing outside the doorway. She introduced her to the other three teachers and their families. "We were just talking about this weather."

"Greg says we could see snow before the end of the week," Al noted, "but you sure couldn't predict that judging by today."

"It is glorious," Beth agreed as she spotted Greg Stone coming across the compound with Amanda.

"Good morning, Greg," Connie called drawing his attention to their small gathering.

He smiled, then glanced at Beth, nodded and headed straight for the church. Amanda hurried along beside him, matching his long strides with three of her own. But Beth saw the little girl look back at her and she thought she saw her smile. Beth was determined not to let another day pass without direct contact with the ranger's daughter. By all indications from the other children, Amanda was a leader in the classroom. It would not be wise to wait until school opened to have her first encounter with Amanda.

Once the service began, Beth knew that she was going to find a spiritual home in Yellowstone. The park chaplain, Harry Dixon, led the services. "Look out these windows," his bass voice boomed. "There before you is all the evidence you'll ever need that there is a God—a living God, a loving God, a God who is not immune to being a bit of a show-off when it comes to His handiwork."

The congregation chuckled, for indeed the sky had never seemed as blue or the clouds as pure white or the mountains as magnificent as they did on this morning.

Reverend Dixon was a silver-haired and silver-tongued dynamo who ran the service as if there would never be enough time in the world to accomplish all of God's work. Beth liked him immediately and counted him among the many blessings she'd already encountered in coming to the park. As she listened to his sermon, she felt such a sense of certainty that coming here was indeed the right choice.

She caught a glimpse of Greg Stone's face as Reverend Dixon made the point that each person was a resident of God's world and in God's care. There was an almost imperceptible tightening of the ranger's jaw, a slight frown that creased his forehead. She recalled something he had said that first night.

"I don't believe in divine intervention, Beth."

She hadn't known about his wife's death then. Now she felt the full impact of those words. Had Greg turned away from his faith when his wife died? If so, why on earth was he standing up there singing in the church choir?

According to Connie, he attended church for Amanda's sake. He was polite to the minister and others, but everyone knew that he had severed all emotional ties with religion the day he buried his wife. As the minister invited everyone to stand for the closing hymn, she studied him closely for further clues. When he stood with the rest of the choir, he focused on the hymnal before him and indeed seemed to be going through the motions of singing rather than paying attention to the words.

Previously, she had only thought of him as tall and somewhat rigid. Now she saw that he had a lean athletic body, skin weathered to a permanent and very attractive tan by days in the outdoors and facial features that were at once fascinating and a little intimidating. She also saw a certain weariness—not physical exhaustion—but something that told her he was worn down mentally and emotionally. Her heart went out to him. She was especially intrigued by the undeniable presence of laugh lines at the corners of his deep-set eyes. Those indelible creases told a story— a story of happier and more carefree times for the oh-so-serious chief ranger.

Beth imagined a younger Greg Stone playing football or perhaps basketball. As an athlete, she'd no doubt that he would have been a fierce competitor. Once the game ended, she wondered, had he put aside his "game face" and celebrated with his teammates, laughing at some joke or ogling the cheerleaders? That kind of easy camaraderie was harder to imagine than the image of him driving for a goal.

She felt sad that he had lost not only his wife, but also the faith that would have helped him endure that loss. Then as she watched, an incredible thing happened. For one of the few times since she's met him, Greg Stone smiled, revealing not only the aforementioned laugh lines but also a most engaging dimple at the corner of his mouth.

Beth followed the line of his gaze to the second row where Amanda stood for the closing hymn. She was making exaggerated hand motions urging him to smile as he stood in the back row of the choir and sang the final verse of the hymn with special gusto.

After church everyone gathered for coffee and cake in celebration of another successful and safe park season.

"In the next few weeks, you won't be seeing much of us, Beth," one of the rangers explained.

Beth was aware that the young man was interested in her. She smiled. "Why is that?"

"Time to shut things down for winter," he replied.

"Yes, this is the last Sunday we'll have the company of our seasonal staff," Connie said as she glanced around the room. "They'll all be heading back to college or their winter jobs," she added with a poignant sigh. "I'll miss them."

Al put his arm around his wife's shoulders. "Connie has this habit of adopting every kid who comes through here," he explained. "She goes through this every year."

"You're the same way with the tourists," she replied. "Al gets so caught up in meeting new people every day during the season that it takes him a while to settle into the quieter routine."

"It's hard to imagine there not being so many tourists around," Beth said recalling how they crowded the streets and how their vehicles lined the main roads. "I must admit that I'm looking forward to that."

"Well, before you know it, we'll be down to a skeletal crew," Al said. "You'll be able to roll a bowling ball down the middle of town here and not hit a thing except maybe a bison," he said wistfully.

"Oh, stop it," Connie chided. "You love the quiet as much as the hubbub and you know it."

Al grinned.

The two of them reminded Beth of her own parents. Their good-natured sparring told the story of a strong marriage, like the one Beth hoped to find for herself some day.

"Well, I for one will be much busier in the week ahead," she said. "School starts tomorrow. I can hardly believe it." Then she grinned sheepishly. "The truth is, I can hardly wait."

"I'm not sure the children share your enthusiasm," Connie replied with a chuckle, nodding toward the place where a group of the older children were watching Beth with barely concealed curiosity and concern.

"Would you folks excuse me?" Beth said with a smile. "I think I have some work to do in putting the children's minds at ease."

Greg Stone worked the room, saying his goodbyes to staff members who would be leaving, touching base with rangers who would manage the schedule of closing facilities during the coming weeks and trying to keep his eye on Amanda.

Ever since Lu had died, he knew he had become overly protective of his daughter. "Dad, I am not a *baby*," Amanda reprimanded him regularly always with a dramatic sigh of exasperation. He would be glad when school started, and he could be sure of her whereabouts for at least the greater part of the day.

He glanced up from his conversation with the park supervisor and saw Amanda standing with three other children, listening to the new teacher. Judging by Beth Baxter's animated hand motions and facial expressions, she was telling quite a tale. The children were fascinated and Greg moved closer to hear what she was saying.

"Well, he was just about the biggest bear I ever saw," Beth said in an awed voice, her hand stretching high over her own petite height. She smiled that smile he had noticed that first night—the one that took over her entire face and seemed to radiate from somewhere deep inside her. "In fact, he was the only bear I'd ever seen outside of a zoo," she added.

"Did he rip open your car?" Dougie Spinner demanded.

Leave it to Dougie to want the graphic details, Greg thought and smiled.

"He tried and he had these long, long fingernails," Beth said curling her own manicured fingers into claws to demonstrate. "He used them to pry and pull and claw at the door." She shuddered at the memory.

"What did you do?" Amanda's best friend, Sara, asked breathlessly.

"My mom said you sang and blew a whistle," Dougie interrupted.

"I did," Beth confirmed.

"She said it must have been just about the worst singing ever heard," Dougie continued. "One of the rangers said if he'd been that bear he would've either run off to the woods or come up on that porch and put you out of your misery."

The children held their collective breaths, suddenly aware that Dougie had repeated gossip he shouldn't have and that the new teacher's feelings were bound to be hurt.

Greg watched and waited.

She laughed. She laughed so hard that the children started to laugh as well. "Your mom was right," Beth confirmed between gulps of laughter. Then she regained control and became quite serious. "Do you want to know a secret?" she asked in a low confidential tone. The children naturally gathered closer and Greg strained to hear. "One of the reasons I had to leave Chicago was because I sang so loud and so bad that the mayor couldn't stand it any more and told me to leave.''

"Chicago's a big place," Sara observed, clearly impressed.

"Not as big as Yellowstone," Dougie declared, equally as determined not to be overly in awe of the new teacher. "You made that part up. So what happened next with the bear?"

"My dad saved her," Amanda announced. It was her first contribution to the animated discussion.

Greg watched as Beth focused her full attention as well as the full radiance of her smile on his daughter. "Yes, he did," she said softly, and added, "Why don't you tell them the rest, Amanda?" In that moment Greg knew that Amanda had been won over, at least for the time being. He stood nearby and listened to his daughter relate the rest of the story even though she had slept through the entire incident. He smiled at her minor embellishment of the facts to make him seem like a real hero.

All the while he was thinking that he liked Beth Baxter a little better for giving his daughter this gift. He looked at her and when her laughing eyes met his, he looked away, confused by feelings stirring deep inside him, feelings that were both faintly familiar and oddly discomforting. Feelings that he had thought were long dead.

Later that night Greg sat on the side of his ten-year-old daughter's bed listening to her prattle on about this and that in an obvious attempt to delay the inevitable. "Amanda, it's time for you to close those big blue eyes and go to sleep," he said gently as he tucked the covers high around her shoulders.

"But, what do you think she'll be like in class, Dad? The new teacher? I like Mrs. Schuller—she's nice. Maybe the new teacher won't be so nice, you know? Just because she *seems* nice doesn't mean anything," she added in the tone she had evidently picked up from listening to adults evaluate a new person.

"The new teacher has a name, and she is only here for a year, Amanda. Mrs. Schuller will be back next year."

"I guess," Amanda agreed reluctantly, "but I don't understand why Mrs. Schuller had to choose this year to go. Next year I'll be going to school in Gardiner with the other big kids."

Greg studied his daughter as he brushed the bangs away from her forehead. Could it possibly be that her concern about the change in teachers went deeper than simply getting used to someone new? Her mother had been dead for well over a year, and while Amanda seemed to have accepted the massive change in both their lives, Greg also knew that he had been too consumed by his own grief in the early months to be much good to his daughter. More recently, his emotions had settled into a kind of dull apathy as he focused every fiber of his life on his work and his daughter's happiness. Could it be that Amanda's questions about the teacher were really about not wanting another unexpected change in her life?

"And why does she have to live right next door?" Amanda said sleepily. "It's bad enough being the kid of the chief ranger without living right next door to the teacher. The other kids will think I'm being given special favors," she groaned.

"It'll work out," Greg promised, knowing he had promised the same thing when Lu had been dying of cancer.

Amanda grunted and pulled her favorite stuffed dog firmly against her chest. "Sure, Dad," she mumbled and then she was asleep.

Greg sat there a minute longer watching his daughter, noticing for the hundredth time the way she curled one arm protectively across her body the way her mother had in sleep. And for the hundredth time he wondered why a God who was supposedly loving and kind would so cruelly take away a mother at a time when her child needed her most. He hoped Beth Baxter would have sense enough to realize that in spite of her lively personality and high intelligence, Amanda was vulnerable. She could be easily hurt. Could someone as obviously inexperienced in the ways of a harder colder world as Beth Baxter was possibly understand that?

Beth could not believe how excited and nervous she was on the opening day of school. Ordinarily, she was not an early morning riser, but she woke before dawn and cooked herself a full breakfast. As she sat on the porch wrapped in a blanket against the chill of the morning and savoring a second cup of coffee, she studied her surroundings.

She had been in Yellowstone less than a week, but already she was beginning to think of it as *home*. She waved to a group of park rangers and naturalists on their way to work and they waved back. There was a real sense of community in living here. One of the other teachers had warned her that like any small town it had its downside. People gossiped and knew more about your comings and goings than was usual in a city, but in spite of that everyone she had met had told her that they would not want to live anywhere else.

Beth heard the now familiar squeak of the screen door on Greg Stone's place as it opened and closed. "Good morning," she said softly not wanting to wake Amanda.

He turned, clearly surprised to see her. "You're up early," he observed.

She grinned. "Couldn't sleep. I never can the first day. Anyway, now I'm kind of glad. It's been wonderful sitting out here in the quiet watching the sunrise."

Greg glanced at the sun and frowned. "Thunderstorms coming this afternoon," he said.

Beth followed his gaze across a cloudless sky. "How on earth can you tell that from a sky so purely blue?"

He held up a sheaf of papers he held in one hand. "Overnight weather reports," he told her. She thought she saw a hint of a smile, but then immediately he frowned. "You do know, Beth, that thunderstorms can be quite sudden and dangerous here in the park? They can come up without warning—even on a day like this. Anyone out in the back country can be caught completely unaware."

"I thought I would let the children get one day in the classroom under their belts before dragging them to the outback," Beth said dryly, wondering if she would ever have a conversation with the ranger that did not involve a lecture.

"It's not like Chicago where you can dash into a building for cover," he continued. "Here, you're exposed to the elements."

"No, it's not like Chicago at all," she replied dreamily as she sipped her coffee. "I can't tell you how wonderful and free I feel here. And how welcome people have made me feel."

"You must miss your friends," he said.

"Of course. But what's happening between me and the people here is unlike anything I've ever experienced." She saw that he was skeptical of her enthusiasm. "No, really, I mean it. All my life I've always had to assess whether someone was being nice to me because they liked me or because they wanted to be closer to my family, or more specifically, my family's money. Here, that's not even a consideration."

"People here are well aware of your family's wealth," he said quietly.

"But that's the point—they know and it's just a fact like that I come from Chicago or that you're their boss. It doesn't mean that's who *you* are as a person."

She realized that her normal penchant for openly sharing her thoughts and feelings was making him distinctly uncomfortable.

He cleared his throat as if preparing to make a speech. "The original topic was storms, Beth, and how you will need to conduct yourself should you and the children—"

She sighed. The man had clearly missed his calling. He was a born professor with a natural talent for lecturing. "I have an idea," she replied. "Whenever I take the children out on a field trip, we'll make sure that you or one of the other rangers are along with us. How would that be?"

"Could you, Dad?" Amanda asked excitedly as she came out onto the porch still in her pajamas. "That would be so cool."

"I certainly want to involve the parents as much as possible in the educational activities of the children," Beth continued, taking some pleasure in watching Greg struggle with his determination to refuse her and his unwillingness to disappoint his daughter.

"Come on, Dad. Say you'll do it," Amanda urged.

"We'll see," Greg replied. Then he lifted his daughter high in his arms and grinned. "Is this what you've chosen to wear for the first day of school, young lady? Because, frankly, I would have thought your new chinos would be so-o-o cool."

Amanda giggled with delight as her father carried her back inside the house. "Aw, Dad, sometimes you are so weird."

Beth swallowed the last of her coffee and listened to the excited and muffled chatter of the child getting ready for school. She heard the clang of dishes and pans as Greg prepared breakfast and heard his bass replies to Amanda's constant stream of questions and commentary. She remembered the way his face had softened and lit with love when he had lifted his daughter and teased her into laughter in that brief moment on the porch. It was the second time that Beth had caught a glimpse of another side of the frequently austere, unsmiling ranger. It was a side of him that at the moment only Amanda seemed able to reach, but one that was definitely intriguing.

Chapter Four

Beth hadn't been in the classroom more than an hour when she realized that she had underestimated the challenge of teaching two different grades in one classroom. She had those children in fifth and sixth grade while the rest of the teachers handled those children from kindergarten through fourth grade. She felt a bit like a pioneer schoolmarm, only these children were definitely modern-day students wise beyond their years to the ways of adults. Fortunately, they were mostly well behaved although the older ones were unable to hide the fact that they had serious concerns about Beth's ability to live up to Mrs. Schuller's standards.

Doug Spinner tested her once or twice by causing disruptions when her back was turned. She handled the situation by asking Doug to take charge of the slower reading group in completing exercises in comprehension while she worked at getting the other children settled into projects. To her delight, it worked. Back in Chicago her directions would have been met with a dramatic sigh or worse, further testing of the boundaries. But Doug's innate politeness and respect for adults kicked in immediately. He herded the youngsters to one corner of the room, passed out workbooks and pencils and strolled back and forth checking their work as if he'd been teaching for years.

During recess Amanda and some of the other children were kicking a soccer ball around. As it came rolling toward Beth, she automatically trapped it and sent it on its way back to the group then returned to writing down ideas that she hoped would make her classroom routine function more smoothly.

"Miss Baxter?"

Amanda stood before her, the soccer ball lodged firmly under one arm. "Do you play soccer?" she asked squinting in the bright sunlight.

"I played in college," Beth said.

"Could you teach us?" Doug chimed in as he edged closer.

Beth was surprised. In Chicago, soccer was the sport of the day for most boys and girls. In many neighborhoods it had largely replaced Little League baseball and football in popularity. "I could try," Beth agreed.

"Al-l-l right," Doug murmured pumping one fist.

"We'll have to work out a time schedule for practices," Beth reminded them. "Why don't you hold a team meeting during the afternoon recess and come up with a plan?''

''We don't have a team,'' Amanda said. ''There's just the three of us,'' nodding toward Doug and Sara.

''I see.'' Beth pretended to consider the situation. ''So, you're telling me that Jeffrey Thompson and the Quentin twins aren't interested?'' She glanced toward the other three older children from the class. Jeffrey was a shy bookworm type, definitely unathletic with his glasses and overweight frame. The Quentin twins were eleven-year-old girls whose interests seemed to run exclusively to hairstyles, clothes and boys—not necessarily in that order. The object of their affection at the moment was clearly Doug Spinner.

Doug's eyes grew large with amazement. ''They don't play,'' he protested.

''So, am I to understand that you've invited them to participate and they've said they'd rather not?'' Beth watched the exchange of looks between Doug, Amanda and Sara, saw them struggle with an answer.

''We never asked,'' Amanda admitted finally.

''I'll do it,'' Sara volunteered eager to please. She took off across the small schoolyard before either Amanda or Doug could stop her. Doug gave an audible groan.

''You know, I really hope they agree to play,'' Beth said. ''It will be so much more fun if we can have a real game, three-on-three, don't you think? I was thinking that for starters the two of you ought to be appointed captains since you already have some knowledge of the game. Also, keep in mind that some of the children from other classes may want to join in.''

"We get to choose players?'' Amanda asked.

"For starters,'' Beth agreed. ''Assuming they want to play.''

"I take Sara,'' Amanda announced immediately.

"No fair,'' Doug challenged.

"Yes, fair. Now you pick,'' Amanda retorted obviously pleased with herself.

"Then you have to take Jeffrey too,'' Doug argued.

Amanda beamed. "Okay. I guess that leaves you with the Quentin twins.'' Then she giggled. ''They're going to *love* that, Dougie,'' she teased as she ran back to the classroom.

Beth suppressed a smile. Amanda Stone was one bright little girl. It was going to be a real joy having her in class.

"How was school?'' Greg asked later that day as Amanda set the table and he stirred the spaghetti sauce.

"Okay,'' she replied with a noncommittal shrug.

"Small class this year,'' Greg commented knowing that this was one of the years when the school board had elected to combine classes to cope with the lower enrollment. Next year Amanda would attend classes in Gardiner where the class size would be more normal.

"Miss Baxter is going to teach us soccer,'' Amanda said.

"Really?'' His calm reply was in direct competition with the flood of thoughts that raced through his mind. In the first place, he had promised to teach Amanda soccer, but with his work schedule and various crises to handle over the past couple of months, he'd kept putting her off. He wondered how many times he was going to disappoint his daughter as he struggled to be both mother and father plus manage the largest national park in the continental U.S. In the second place, Beth Baxter—in spite of her appearance of fitness—did not seem like the type who would engage in a sport like soccer. She might chip those perfectly polished nails.

"She's pretty cool," Amanda continued as she put the hot garlic bread in a basket and set it on the table. Then she giggled.

"What?" Greg asked, smiling at his daughter's obvious amusement.

"She made me and Dougie captains of the soccer teams—that means we got to choose up sides. I chose Sara, of course."

"Of course," Greg said trying hard to think who else might be available to take part in a team sport. "Who did Doug choose?"

Amanda crowed with laughter. "That's the best part. When I took Sara, he got mad and said I had to take Jeffrey Thompson so he was left with…" She was laughing so hard she simply couldn't get the words out.

"Well, don't keep me in suspense. Who's on Dougie's team?"

"The Quentin twins."

Greg immediately saw the reason for his daughter's delight. The Quentin girls had shadowed Doug Spinner for the better part of the summer. If Doug was around, one or both of them was sure to be nearby. No matter what the poor kid did, he could not shake those two adoring females. Greg laughed with Amanda.

"Miss Baxter really is pretty cool," Amanda repeated once she had gotten control of her mirth and turned her attention back to her spaghetti. "I think she'll do fine."

Greg knew that for his daughter, this was tantamount to declaring that Beth Baxter was the greatest thing since sliced bread. "Well, if you need some help with soccer, things have started to quiet down now. I have some time."

Amanda's eyes lit with delight. "Really? Can I go tell Miss Baxter after supper? I mean like you could coach one team and she could coach the other and it would be the most funnest thing. Of course, you should probably coach Dougie's team. He's going to need a *lot* of help." This last sent her into a fresh wave of laughter, and Greg thought that it had been too long since he and Amanda had shared such a wonderful time together. It crossed his mind that in one sense he had Beth to thank for providing the fodder for this moment.

By the end of her first week of teaching in Yellowstone, Beth was beginning to rethink the idea that she had made a wise choice in coming. The leisurely pleasure of time to enjoy the park, to wave to her neighbors and to fantasize about what her life would become had changed dramatically. She spent long hours at the school and at home adapting lesson plans to the needs of these children. Recently she'd been so busy that she'd barely had time to see her neighbors or any adults at all. What had seemed like a decision blessed by the angels as she sat on her front stoop that first morning had quickly become one that was colored by innumerable doubts.

For one thing, she daily realized how little she really knew about living outside of a city environment. The children seemed to know more about the plants and animals than she did, and she found herself staying up half the night memorizing facts and preparing lessons in order to stay two steps ahead of them. She took her teaching seriously and was concerned that her lack of knowledge would somehow rob the children of a level of teaching she thought they deserved.

On top of that, she was a little lonely. It wasn't that the other residents weren't warm and friendly. It was that they were so busy with their own lives. Their work demanded enormous dedication. Connie sympathized and reminded Beth that in a place like Yellowstone, the permanent staffers were used to seeing people come and go. They were aware that Beth would only be in the park for this one season.

"Just wait until everything finally settles down for the winter," Connie assured her. "That's when things start hopping in town here—lectures, concerts, book discussion groups and amateur theater. Honey, you'll

start to wish you could find a few minutes to yourself.''

Beth thought about Greg, who certainly didn't
seem to mind being alone when he wasn't working.
He always came straight home from work regardless
of what hour that might be. Once or twice she had
been outside her unit or on her way home from catching up on some work at school when he came home.
He was always polite, but never seemed inclined to
want to stop and visit as others did. She thought again
about inviting him and Amanda over for supper, but
wondered how such an invitation might be read—by
the ranger and by others in the small tightknit community. Also, she didn't want to put Amanda in the
awkward position of appearing to be receiving special
attention.

At Connie's suggestion, Beth had asked Sandy
Quentin to tutor her on the wildlife and plants of the
park. Sandy was a naturalist for the park system and
her husband Sam had happily given up the practice
of law to run a hardware store in Gardiner. She was
also a born matchmaker sprinkling each session liberally with hints that this ranger or that naturalist was
certainly eligible and would be a great catch if Beth
would be at all interested. Beth began to understand
why the Quentin twins might be so interested in boys.
Their mother was always trying to pair Beth up with
one of her single friends.

To Beth's surprise, whenever Sandy brought up the
idea of her dating someone in the park, the face that
came to her mind was that of Greg Stone. She actually

found herself holding back from asking questions about him, not wanting Sandy to think she was interested. As Connie had warned her, living in Yellowstone was like living in any small town, and Sandy was a charming but eager gossip. Beth knew that all it would take was for her to ask one question about the rugged chief ranger and rumors would spread like wildfire. She told herself that her fascination with Greg was his close proximity in living in the other half of the house and at the same time the clear message he gave off that it was best she keep her distance.

Unlike her father, Amanda was another story entirely. With each passing day, the little girl became more fascinated by Beth. She often came to school early and stayed late to help with the setup of materials and the cleanup afterward. At times like this she would chatter away about whatever might be on her mind. Her conversation was liberally sprinkled with phrases like "Mom used to always say…" or "Before Mom died…" as if it were perfectly normal for a child's mother to die so young.

The first time Amanda had mentioned her mother, Beth had been quick to say how sorry she was and she'd been racking her brain for something appropriate to add about why such things sometimes happen even to wonderful little girls like Amanda. Instead, it was Amanda who comforted her.

"Don't be sad," she had said. "I was sad for a very long time, but now that I'm older I understand that God sometimes needs a special person like Mom. He wouldn't have taken her unless He really really needed her, and He must have figured that Dad and I could manage okay on our own—at least until He and Mom decide on someone new.''

''Someone new?''

Amanda had nodded firmly. ''Oh, yes. Reverend Dixon told me that he was very sure that one day someone would come along and me, Dad and the new lady would be a whole family again.'' She had smiled at the thought. ''And the best part is that I'll know Mom picked this lady specially for us. That kind of thing takes time, you know.''

Beth had resisted asking what Amanda's father thought of all this. She had also marveled at the wisdom of the park chaplain in finding a way to explain the unexplainable in terms that would be comforting and acceptable to a ten-year-old. She wondered if he'd been able to offer anything approaching the same level of comfort to Greg.

One evening as she left the school after her session with Sandy, Beth saw Greg working a soccer ball back and forth with Amanda and Doug across the playground. She put down her books and walked across to the field for a closer look.

''Concentrate, Amanda,'' Greg called to his daughter whose face was a portrait of focused intensity as she worked the ball with her feet. ''Defense, Doug,'' he coached. ''She's coming for your goal.''

Beth grimaced as Doug aggressively went after the ball, but Amanda held her own, jostling him, turning her body with natural athletic instinct to protect the ball. Beth resisted the urge to cheer. When Amanda finally lost control of the ball it rolled straight toward Beth.

"Toss it here, Miss Baxter," Doug shouted waving his hands.

"Oh, goody, now we can play teams," Amanda shouted. "Come on, Miss Baxter, girls against guys."

"I don't think…" Greg began.

"You don't think what, Chief?" Beth shouted over her shoulder as she began working the ball toward the goal at Doug's end of the field. Admittedly it was a bit more difficult controlling the ball as she ran in a jumper that reached her ankles than it would have been in jeans. Still, she was determined to give it her best effort.

"Come on, Ranger Stone," Doug cried as he dashed after her. "She's gonna score."

Amanda gave a whoop of delight and came running alongside Beth. Beth grinned down at her and in that split second Greg was right there in front of her stealing the ball and heading for the opposite end of the field. She couldn't be sure but she thought he had actually chuckled at his clever maneuver.

"Not so fast, hotshot," she muttered as she caught up with him from behind and kicked the ball cleanly away and toward Amanda. "Go, Amanda," she shouted and laughed at the expression of total shock on Greg Stone's face.

"Mom, Dad," Doug shouted as he spotted his own parents on his way down the field to catch Amanda. "Come on."

In minutes it was a three-on-three game, women against men. Connie Spinner was a crafty player, and she easily manipulated the ball into position for Amanda to score the first goal. The air was punctuated by the excited shrieks of the three females as they danced and high-fived one another in the middle of the field.

"Aw, Dad, you let her get by you," Doug moaned.

Al Spinner ruffled his son's close-cropped hair. "It's getting dark, son, and I imagine you've got homework." He glanced over at Beth and raised one questioning eyebrow.

"He certainly does," Beth said. "Book report," she reminded him.

"Oh, man," Doug muttered and trudged off the field with his parents.

"Hey, Dougie, you want to stay for pizza with me and Dad?" Amanda took off after her friend, leaving Greg and Beth alone in the center of the field.

"I've noticed that Amanda is always watching out for the other children," Beth said when the silence seemed to stretch too long for comfort but neither of them had moved.

"Yeah, she's a terrific kid," Greg agreed.

"It's a very adult thing for her to do," Beth added.

"She's had to grow up fast," Greg said and his tone left no doubt that there was no point in pursuing the conversation.

The sun had set and in the gathering shadows she couldn't read his expression. "Well, it's getting late," she said bending over to pick up the ball. When she handed it to him, their fingers brushed and it seemed like so much more than a simple touch. Beth told herself that she was reading too much into an innocent and perfectly natural gesture.

"Did you eat?" he asked.

Suddenly she felt like an awkward teenager, unable to find her voice. She shook her head and waited for the invitation she very much hoped would come.

"Hey, Spinners," Greg shouted across the field. "Come on in. There's plenty of pizza." He started toward the duplex. The Spinner family and Amanda came from the opposite direction. Beth remained standing in the middle of the playing field. "You coming or not?" Greg asked.

"Oh, you mean that invitation included me even though my name is Baxter not Spinner?" she teased.

"Well, if you need an engraved invitation..."

"Nope. I never turn down food especially when somebody else is cooking. You *are* cooking, aren't you?" She fell into step alongside him. "I just hope you're a better cook than you are a soccer player," she added after a moment.

He actually chuckled. "You know I let you win," he said.

"No way."

Greg watched Beth make herself at home in his kitchen. He listened to her easy banter with Connie and Al, heard the sound of her laughter invading the silence of his house. He smelled the scent of her perfume as she sat next to him eating pizza. When a bit of tomato sauce caught on her lower lip, he thought about wiping it away, touching her and recalled the way their fingers had touched when she handed him the soccer ball. He shook off such fantasies and tried to concentrate on anything else—anybody else. For someone so petite, she certainly knew how to fill up a room.

After everyone had devoured the pizza, Beth and Connie insisted on clearing the dishes and they were soon engrossed in conversation about teaching. Amanda came up to Beth to ask a question about Chicago, and Greg watched as Beth reached out and tucked an errant strand of hair behind his daughter's ear. That simple gesture—so natural, so tender—drew him to her more than anything he'd seen her do or heard her say. Something about her natural instinct to nurture his daughter touched Greg deeply and roused emotions he had suppressed for months. For the rest of the evening he felt shy and uncertain around her, unable to meet her eyes in the normal course of the evening's adult conversation. He was grateful for the buffer of Al and Connie.

He told himself that he was grateful when the evening ended early, and at the same time wondered why he was trying to think of a reason for her to stay. Connie and Al were anxious to get Doug home to finish his book report, and Beth took the opportunity to leave as well. Greg saw Amanda look at him, and knew that she wanted the teacher to stay.

"Amanda and I were glad for the company," he said in answer to everyone's chorus of appreciation for the pizza. He walked with them all to the door and watched as Al and Doug headed across the compound while Connie stopped to finish a conversation with Beth. "Good night," he said.

The two women looked at him and smiled. Greg stepped back inside and closed the door.

"Do you like Miss Baxter?" Amanda asked.

"Sure. She's a nice lady." He thought about her touching Amanda's hair.

"I mean, do you *like* her?"

"Why do you ask?" Greg hedged, banning the memory of the woman's tenderness from his mind. He knew where Amanda's line of questioning was headed, and it was not a topic he was prepared to discuss.

Amanda studied him for a minute, then shrugged. "No reason," she said and started clearing the last of the dessert dishes.

"I'll do that, honey. Finish your homework and get your shower. You need to wash your hair tonight."

"My homework's all done."

"Then go take your shower while I clean up here."

Amanda headed for her room. "I like her more and more and I think Mom would like her, too," she said softly but loud enough so that he couldn't miss it.

Greg frowned as he listened to the sounds of Amanda in the shower and dried the last of the glasses. Beth Baxter was slowly but surely worming her way into his daughter's heart. It wasn't that he thought she had any diabolical intention but the fact remained that Amanda was drawn to her in a way that was different from her attachment to any other adult. The problem as he saw it continued to be the fact that Beth was here for the school year and then she'd be gone. Amanda had already lost her mother. It wouldn't do for her to become attached to Beth and have her leave, too. Letting go of someone you loved hurt too much—he ought to know.

Clearly, Amanda had other ideas about the role that Miss Baxter was to play in their lives. As he combed the tangles out of her freshly washed hair, she chattered on and on about things at school—things that largely had Beth's name coming up every other sentence.

"So, I told her that you'd be glad to help out. You will, won't you, Dad?"

He'd been lost in his own thoughts. "Will what, honey?" He braided the top section of Amanda's thick hair, one more skill he had acquired since Lu's death.

Amanda gave an exasperated sigh and rolled her eyes. "Come to class and talk about plants and animals and stuff."

"The naturalists usually handle that sort of thing."

"Well, Miss Baxter says that she wants to get us in the big classroom before winter comes. Anyway, I told her you would know the very best places to go and that you knew all about every animal in the park. And, that you could name most every tree and flower, too."

"What's the big classroom?"

"The park, Dad. Miss Baxter says it would be a

crime to be surrounded by all this nature and spend all day inside a stupid building—well, she didn't say *stupid building*. She was telling us today all about the big fire that happened before any of us were even born. She showed us awesome pictures. I bet you know all about that, don't you, Dad?''

"Come on, Amanda, it's time for bed." He held back the covers for her. He'd been only twenty-two years old when the fire had raged through the park in 1988. Nothing the rangers and volunteers did seemed to work. He remembered the heat and the devastation as if it had all happened yesterday.

"You just *have* to come talk to the class," Amanda pleaded as she climbed into bed and settled a lineup of stuffed animals for the night. "I promised and Mom told me it was really awful to break a promise."

"We'll see, honey. It's late. Get some sleep."

"Miss Baxter said she was pretty sure that you knew everything there was to know about the fire and anything else that had to do with the park, so will you do it?" Amanda looked up at him to see if her words had had any effect. "She said I should ask you and she said it would be wonderful if you agreed. She said it just like that—*wonderful*."

He leaned over and kissed her. "I'll check my schedule."

"I'll tell Miss Baxter to come see you in your office or maybe we should just have her come over for supper again. That was a lot of fun, huh, Dad?"

"I'll talk to Miss Baxter. You go to sleep."

"She's real pretty, don't you think, Dad?"

"Sleep," he repeated and shut out the light.

It didn't take a genius to see what was happening. His daughter was matchmaking, which might have been harmless enough if she wasn't going to be disappointed in the process. Women like Beth Baxter came to Yellowstone for an adventure—not for a life. In June she would pack up and return to Chicago where no doubt she'd be relieved to get back to her normal routine and where he was certain there must be a line of rich young stockbroker types just waiting to make their move.

Greg sat down at his desk to finish a report. Lu's photograph stared back at him. He picked it up and studied it, feeling a twinge of disloyalty that lately he'd been thinking so much about Beth Baxter. The one thing he had promised Lu was that he would take care of Amanda and do everything in his power to protect her from ever being hurt again. Lu had laughed at him and reminded him that God was in charge and there wasn't much Greg could do about that.

Was that when he had first realized that his faith was reduced to little more than going through the motions? Was it the day his dying wife had reminded him that God was in charge? Was that the first time he had swallowed his protest that there was no God in deference to her need to believe that there was?

He replaced the photograph on his desk and stared at it from a distance. He stood up and walked the short distance next door before he could lose his nerve. Greg didn't have much use for a God who took a vibrant woman in the prime of her life for no good reason. He wasn't about to put any faith in a God who would leave Amanda without a mother. And most of all, he wondered what kind of cruel joke God was playing now by sending a woman like Beth into his life to make him feel things he didn't want to feel and then have her leave again.

Chapter Five

"**W**e have to talk," Greg said without preamble when she answered the door. "Is this a good time?" He tried to ignore the way she had pushed her glasses onto the top of her head, how she was barefoot and it made her seem even smaller and more vulnerable. She opened the door a little wider as an invitation for him to come inside.

Greg felt confusion at the emotions she stirred. Because he was a man determined to maintain control of his emotions, that confusion irritated him. Going inside her place seemed far too intimate a gesture. He backed away from the open door. "If you don't mind, could we talk on the porch here? I just put Amanda to bed and in case she needs me…" he finished lamely.

"Sure. I'll get a jacket," Beth replied.

"And shoes," he said. "It's cooled off quite a bit."

She glanced at her feet and grinned. "Good idea," she said.

Greg returned to his side of the porch and waited. She appeared a couple of minutes later wrapped in a heavy hand-knit woolen sweater and wearing, not shoes but slippers that came to her ankles and were shaped like the face of a bear at the toes. He recognized them as one of the items sold at the town store to the tourists.

She lifted one foot so he could get a better look. "Appropriate? Wouldn't you say? Connie gave them to me one day when I was feeling a little homesick."

He frowned. She wasn't going to make this easy for him. Her quirky smile and habit of sharing the minor details of her life with such abandon turned his resolve as well as his knees to jelly.

"Amanda wants me to come talk to the class," he began.

"That would be wonderful," Beth replied as she hoisted herself onto the porch railing to sit.

"I'll come on one condition," he continued.

"Okay, Chief Ranger," she replied in a deep bass voice that mocked his attempt to keep the conversation on a serious plane. "What are your terms?"

This was not going at all the way he had expected. He cleared his throat and paced the confines of the small porch. "I'm sure you're aware that my daughter likes…admires you very much."

Silence.

"I'm sure you also know that her mother died recently, and that given that fact she is still pretty fragile, pretty impressionable, pretty..." He searched for the right word.

"Spit it out, Greg," Beth said but her voice was tense and she wasn't kidding around now.

Greg tried another tack. "As you observed earlier this evening, Amanda is fairly precocious. Since her mother died, she has taken on a great deal of responsibility. One of the things she has focused on is taking care of me." He cleared his throat again. "Tonight, it occurred to me that given her admiration of you and her desire to see me happy, she might...that is, she has gotten it into her head that perhaps you...and I... I mean, it's completely ridiculous, of course, but I have to protect my daughter, you understand."

The woman was not helping one bit. He was fairly certain that she knew exactly what he was trying to say, however badly, yet she remained as still as Yellowstone Canyon on a winter day.

"Now you listen to me, Chief Ranger Stone," she finally said in a low and dangerously soft tone. "I am quite capable of recognizing Amanda's infatuation with me. I am also sensitive enough to understand that for a little girl who has recently lost her mother the hope that someday there might be a chance that you and she might find someone new is perfectly normal. I know that you think the worst of me, but let me assure you that I like your daughter very much and I would never willingly do anything to hurt her. You can count on me to nip any fantasy she may have of you and me as a couple in the bud." She hopped off the railing and headed toward her front door, then turned and stood at mock attention. "Will there be anything else, sir?"

He'd handled the whole thing badly. "I didn't mean to imply…"

"If there's nothing else, I'll say good-night," she replied.

"One more thing," he called after her just before she shut the door. "I can be in class on Tuesday morning if that works for you?"

"It doesn't," she replied and shut the door firmly.

He showed up anyway and rather than make a scene, Beth made a great fuss over the honor of having the chief ranger as their guide.

"Yellowstone is the largest of the national parks outside of Alaska," Greg said by way of introduction. "It covers 2.2 million acres with 1,200 miles of trails, over 3,000 miles of rivers and streams and 10,000 thermal features."

"What's a *termal* feature?" One of the fifth graders asked.

"Mud pots, geysers. That stuff," replied Doug Spinner.

"Are we gonna see a geyser today, Chief Ranger Stone?" the Quentin twins asked in unison.

Greg looked disconcerted by the manner in which the children had taken charge of the discussion. Clearly he had expected them to sit like little robots and listen politely and attentively to his prepared remarks.

"Let's give the chief ranger a chance to tell us

what he wants us to know and then ask questions, children," Beth said.

Ten eager faces turned their attention from their teacher back to him and waited.

"Perhaps it would be interesting for the children to know about the animals in the park," Beth suggested.

Greg cleared his throat and nodded. He clasped his hands behind him and paced up and down in front of the children seated on the grass. "There are approximately 30,000 elk, 2,200 bison, a thousand or so mule deer, 700 moose, 400 antelope, 600 bighorn sheep, 200 grizzlies plus coyote, otter, beaver and, of course, the wolf population we've reintroduced to the park over the last decade."

Beth saw the children's eyes glazing over as he inundated them with numbers. "Well, children, that certainly gives us a lot to look for. As we travel today you may also wish to watch for the wonderful variety of birds that populate the park. Can anyone name one of those?"

"Bald eagle," Doug shouted.

"Trumpeter swan," Amanda added.

"Osprey," said the fifth grader with the lisp, spraying his neighbor in the process.

"Loon," chorused the Quentin twins and then they giggled.

"Very good," Beth said enthusiastically. "Now, let's go see what we can find and, along the way, we'll also take a good look at the flowers and the trees." She herded the children into the van she had borrowed for the day. "Coming?" she asked as Greg stood rooted to the spot where he had begun his lecture.

Without a word he climbed into the passenger seat.

"Seat belts everyone," Beth called out and was rewarded by a chorus of metallic clicks. "Buddy check," she called and each child reported in the name of his or her buddy for the day. "And we're off," she said cheerfully as she shifted the van into gear and lurched forward. "Sorry about that," she told Greg. "It's been a while since I drove a stick."

"Now remember, children, there are rules if we are lucky enough to spot wildlife while we're out on the trail. What are they?"

"No closer than twenty-five yards," the children chanted, "except for a bear is no closer than a hundred yards."

"And how far is that?" Beth asked.

"A lon-n-g way," the children replied solemnly.

"Perhaps you have some fun facts you might share with the children as we spot various species, Chief Ranger," she said as she navigated the twisting road.

"Fun facts?"

"You know, things they can relate to and therefore, will remember. Like there's a herd of bison—tell us a fun fact about them." She pulled into an overlook and pointed out the herd grazing in the field.

"Bison may look slow and clumsy but even though they weigh nearly a ton—two thousand pounds—they can run at thirty miles per hour. That's three times as fast as a person can run." He looked to her for approval.

She smiled. "Very good."

Gradually he got the hang of interacting with the children. Beth saw that he was both surprised and pleased at their questions and curiosity. She saw that when he permitted himself to loosen up he was funny and a natural teacher. He came up with quizzes for the children as they rode from one point to another in the park. At the geyser basin he made them each choose a time when they thought the geyser would erupt and then clocked it on his watch. Before her very eyes he relaxed and enjoyed not only the children but also the opportunity to show off the park. It was undeniable that the park held a very special place in his heart.

Their last stop before heading home was a meadow where Greg told them the story of the fire of 1988 and then showed them why the fire had turned out to be such a good thing for the park. He showed them the new growth, the rebirth of plant species that had been overshadowed by the more mature growth of the forest.

"You see children," Beth concluded, "here in the park, there is birth and death and rebirth just as there is in life. The fires seemed a horrible thing when they happened. Yet here we can see that they brought something new and necessary, and that something good came out of this terrible thing."

The children nodded solemnly. Beth looked at Greg to see his reaction realizing that he might have thought she was trying to deliver some message about his anger over Lu's death.

He stared at her for a long moment and then handed her the bouquet of wildflowers he had collected to explain the different species to the children. "Thanks for letting me come along today," he said.

Beth's hand shook as she accepted the flowers. "Our pleasure," she replied softly.

Beth was already in her fourth week of teaching and once she had gotten past that early spat of loneliness, she had settled quickly into a routine that was both rewarding and rigorous.

"Hi, Beth." Al Spinner caught up with her as she walked the short distance from the school to her duplex.

"Hi, Al. How are things going for you?"

Al smiled. "Pretty quiet these days with most of the tourists gone. Connie wanted me to ask you if you'd lead the discussion at tonight's book group? She's got a frog in her throat and can barely squawk much less lead a discussion."

"I'm not sure I'm the right person, Al. I'm new to the group and—"

"Have you read it?"

"Several times," Beth admitted.

"Then you're elected. See you at eight. I'll bring the brownies."

"Now you're bribing me," Beth called after him.

Al waved and continued on his way. Beth turned and realized Greg Stone had come up behind her.

"Hi," she said and her voice was unsteady.

"Hello." He continued to stand there.

"Are you coming to the discussion tonight?"

"Are you leading it?" he asked.

She wondered what the right answer might be to get him to say that he would be there. In the end she settled for the truth. "It looks that way. Connie has a sore throat."

"Then I'll be there." He stepped aside to allow her to pass before heading in the opposite direction toward his office.

"It's at eight," she called after him. "In the meeting room at the admin building."

He nodded and waved but did not break stride.

Beth stood watching him all the way across the compound, her books clutched to her chest like a lovestruck teen.

The meeting room filled quickly with a dozen members of the book discussion group. Beth took her place on one side of the circle of chairs and glanced around. He wasn't there. He had probably started working on some report and lost track of the time.

Al called the group to order and dispensed with two short items of business. "And with that, my dear Beth, the floor is yours."

Beth shuffled her notes and smiled at the others. It struck her that several of the people surrounding her had already become good friends. It was hard to believe how quickly the time had flown since her first days in the park. Back in Chicago her family and friends eagerly awaited the tales of her latest adventure.

She began the discussion by providing background information about the author and the writing of the novel that many critics thought was his finest work. Then she launched the discussion.

"I thought tonight that it might be interesting to begin our discussion by talking, not about Bill Cobb, the protagonist, but about his wife."

The door at the back of the room opened and closed. Greg nodded to the others as he took a chair on the fringe of the circle and focused his attention on her.

"What would you say is her primary emotion throughout the novel?" Beth asked trying to ignore Greg's gaze riveted on her.

"Hopeless hope," he said quietly.

"Well, she was hopeful—I wouldn't necessarily say hopeless," Connie croaked.

"Hopeless," Greg repeated. "She knew from the opening scene that he was dying and there was nothing she could do to stop that. The best she could do was be there and hold things together."

If he had delivered his comments in a tone of anger, there might have been cause to dismiss them. Instead he stated his thoughts with dispassion and because everyone in the room knew that he was coming from a place they hoped never to have to be, they listened.

Beth swallowed around the lump that had suddenly formed in her throat. Why on earth had they selected this particular book to review? Shouldn't someone have recognized how painful it might be for Greg?

"I think we have to look at this on a larger scale," one of the naturalists said. "I mean, the author is writing about the death of a life-style, of an era."

"That's true," Greg replied, "but the people count, too. This is about a man and his wife and their children coming to grips with the fact that the life they had thought they would have—the life they had planned—will never be."

Beth saw the way his outward calm was betrayed by his clenched hands.

Everyone was silent. Beth had no idea how to direct the discussion.

"What about this business that Bill kept going back to about his own childhood?" Al asked and with some relief the group picked up that thread and followed it.

Greg remained politely attentive but quiet throughout the rest of the discussion. Beth couldn't take her eyes off him. She had read the popular novel more than once and yet she was seeing it entirely differently. She was seeing it through Greg's eyes, through his experience and she began to appreciate in a way she had never been able to before just how traumatic these last two years must have been for him.

When the discussion ended and everyone broke into small groups to enjoy coffee and Al's brownies, Beth approached Greg.

"Thank you," she said and knew it sounded dumb.

He concentrated on stirring his coffee, even though he took it black. "For what?"

"For helping me see something in a new light, for

opening a door on a topic I haven't had the courage to really look at before.''

"You mean *death?*"

She nodded.

He smiled. "Actually I thought I was a little over the top. I think I made a number of my friends uncomfortable and that wasn't fair."

"Maybe they were just surprised to hear you make the connection. Maybe it gave them something new to think about as it did me."

He focused all of his attention on her. "You're a very kind person, Beth Baxter," he said softly. "A good person."

"Do you really think that your wife was without hope?" She knew there was a risk in asking. The progress they had made toward forging a friendship was fragile.

"I wasn't talking about my wife," he replied.

"I know, but now I am. Was she without hope?"

He shrugged. "She did what she needed to do to get her through to the end. And I did—and do—what I need to do to get through the days."

Beth wished there were some way she could make him see that going through his grief alone was the hard way to do it—it would take much longer if he closed his heart to what he was feeling, remembering. From everything she knew about his wife, Beth was positive that Lu would not have wanted this for Greg.

Chapter Six

~

Beth was putting the finishing touches on the crib quilt she was making for her best friend's first baby. A week had passed since the discussion group, and she had decided that she might as well face the truth. She had a major crush on the handsome ranger and his gruff exterior was part of the attraction. She could not deny that she watched for Greg as she moved around the compound. She listened for his voice in the evenings. Her radar went up whenever someone mentioned his name. She even worried about him when he was gone for what seemed an unusually long time handling business in some other region of the vast park.

Beth smiled as she held the quilt up to the light to examine it for any flaws or missed stitches. Her friend Ginny had been married for five years and had been trying to have a child for at least four of those years.

Finally it was going to happen. This time in two months, Ginny would be a mother and Beth would be a godmother. Beth couldn't help wondering what it would be like to have a child of her own.

"Beth?" The calling of her name was followed by a sharp knock on the front door.

Beth realized that it had started to rain again. It had been raining off and on all day. She had been so engrossed in her work that she hadn't noticed. Glancing out the window as she hurried to answer the door, she saw that the rain was coming down in sheets.

Connie was standing on her porch, shielding Amanda from the blowing rain. "Come in," Beth urged. "Let me get you a towel."

"I came to ask a favor," Connie called as Beth disappeared into the bathroom and returned with two towels.

"Name it," Beth replied as she knelt to dry Amanda's face and hair.

"Greg is out on the trail somewhere. Amanda was staying with us, but we just got a call that Al's mom has taken a fall up at the ranch in Bozeman. We need to head up there right away. Amanda insists that she can stay at home by herself and wait for him, but I wanted you to know in case you heard her moving around or something. Greg should be home soon—we tried rousing him on the two-way but couldn't get through."

"Is that all right with you, Amanda?" Beth asked. "Staying home alone?"

Teeth chattering as she adjusted to being out of the

rain and cold, Amanda nodded but a flash of lightning made her eyes widen with anxiety. ''I'm not afraid,'' she said with fierce determination that reminded Beth of Greg.

''I tried Sara's folks,'' Connie added, ''but since it's Saturday they've gone off somewhere. I hate to leave her, but—''

''I've got a better idea. Why doesn't Amanda stay here with me? She can keep me company since I'm not real fond of thunderstorms.'' Beth saw that the news surprised Amanda and that the child began to relax. ''You and Al go ahead and give my best to his mom.''

Connie pulled the hood of her rain gear back in place. ''Okay, then it's settled and I'm off.'' Connie bent and kissed Amanda's cheek then hugged Beth. A car horn sounded and Connie opened the door and waved at Al.

''Call when you get there,'' Beth shouted as Connie made a dash for the truck where Al waited. Connie waved again and they were gone.

''Did you make this?'' Amanda asked and Beth turned to find her examining the baby quilt.

''I'm just finishing it. My best friend back in Chicago is going to have a baby in a few weeks. It's my present for the new baby.''

''It's beautiful,'' Amanda said. ''Is it hard to do?'' She was studying the pattern of small colorful squares intently.

''It takes some patience but the fun is in figuring

out what color or pattern to put where. I could show you how," Beth offered.

"You mean I could make one for my bed...for Dad's bed?"

Beth laughed. "Why don't we start with something smaller like a quilt for your doll there and see how it goes?" She motioned to the doll sticking out of the backpack Connie had left by the door.

"Great," Amanda announced as she ran to get the doll.

Beth pulled out her box of leftover quilt squares. "What's your doll's name?"

"Trudy." Amanda immediately began sorting through the fabric. "She doesn't like red but pink is her favorite color."

"How about blue?"

"Blue's good," Amanda agreed. "This is going to be so much fun," she added with a happy grin.

Beth was relieved to see that Amanda was so engrossed in selecting the fabric that she didn't even notice the rumble of thunder coming closer.

Greg Stone was beat. He'd left the house before dawn, and it felt as if he'd been driving for so long that the seat of his truck was permanently welded to his backside. He stretched his shoulders and neck in a futile attempt to relieve some of the tension.

After he'd stopped by the store and found it closed, he headed up the hill to the Spinner house. Al and Connie lived on the outskirts of the town in one of the single-family homes that overlooked the village.

Lu had always wanted to live up there in a house all their own and he had promised her that someday they would. He had promised her a lot of *some days.*

He frowned as he pulled into the Spinner's driveway and saw that the house was as dark as the store had been. *Where were they?*

Knowing Connie's habit of leaving him notes if she couldn't raise him on his cell phone or pager, he left the engine running and made a dash through the pouring rain to the front porch. As predicted a sheet of white paper was taped to the front door. He ripped it free and read it quickly. Amanda was at home. Even though he was less than half a mile from home he dialed the number as he drove back down the winding road.

No answer.

His heart began to beat faster. Amanda was afraid of storms. His hands tightened on the steering wheel. As he turned the corner, he saw that only half the duplex was lit. Amanda wasn't home or if she was, she was sitting in the dark, which wasn't likely. Greg reversed his vehicle and headed back up the hill to where Amanda's friend Sara lived. No one was home there, either.

Fighting the low-grade sense of panic that had become a part of his life since the day he had first realized that he was going to lose Lu and there was nothing he could do to protect her or himself from that, Greg headed for the administration building. Only a skeletal crew remained on duty, and they reported that Connie had called to say that Amanda would be at home.

Where was Amanda?

She must be terrified. Normally a brave little kid, she flinched at every rumble and squeezed her eyes shut at the first flash of lightning. If the storm came at night, she would come into his room and huddle in bed next to him. It was night and the storm was raging and she was nowhere to be found. In addition to his panic, he felt a sense of anger at himself for his own inadequacies in trying to be both parent to Amanda and manager of the park.

Greg left the administration building and headed back to his own house. Maybe there was a message from Amanda. Maybe she had gone off with her friend Sara and her family. Maybe…

He pulled the truck to a halt at the back of the duplex and made a dash for the back door. Lights blazed in Beth's place. He could see her standing at her kitchen sink. She was laughing and talking to somebody.

"Whoa! Major steal," she shouted loud enough for him to actually hear her through the slightly open window. Amanda had told him that Beth was a firm believer in fresh air no matter what the temperature.

The thunder followed seconds later and as he fumbled with the keys to his own back door, he heard a second voice yell, "Go-o-al!" in perfect imitation of the announcer at the Olympic soccer games. This was punctuated by a most familiar giggle.

Greg gulped air as he realized that he could breathe

again. Amanda was safe. Not only that, but she was actually cheering and enjoying a thunderstorm. He walked closer to the window and looked in.

There was Beth stirring cookie dough and talking to Amanda who was perched on a high stool sewing something, her tongue firmly locked in one corner of her mouth as she concentrated on the work. It was a scene of domestic bliss that might have come straight off of a Norman Rockwell calendar. To Greg's amazement the wetness on his face wasn't all due to the rain. He swiped at tears.

Beth glanced up to see if there was another flash of lightning coming and looked straight into the eyes of Greg Stone. She screamed and dropped the cookie pan. Fortunately it was empty. "You scared the day-lights out of me," she said as she rushed to open her back door and usher him inside.

"Sorry," Greg mumbled as he shrugged out of his rain slicker and let her take it while he pulled off his soaked boots.

"Daddy!" Amanda caught him in a bear hug around his waist. "Come see what Beth taught me. I'm a quilter," she announced proudly.

"Miss Baxter," he corrected automatically as he permitted his daughter to pull him along to the counter where she had left her sewing.

"I told Amanda that in situations like this one, it would be okay to call me Beth. I hope that's not a problem."

"No, I... Wow, that's really something, sweetheart," Greg said studying the uneven stitching and matching of the fabric squares.

"It's a quilt for my doll," Amanda explained not waiting for his obvious question. "See, Beth made this one for her baby godchild that's going to be born in a few weeks." Amanda held up the crib quilt, then dropped it and ran to the sofa. "And, not only that but her very own grandmother made this great big one here. It's called a crazy quilt. Isn't it just the coolest thing you ever saw?"

"Very nice," Greg said. He glanced around the room as if he had suddenly stepped into a foreign world. He had never actually been inside her half of the duplex since that first night when he'd helped her unload her car. It was a totally different place.

"Did you get my note?" Beth asked.

"Your note?"

"We left a note on the front door and by the phone at your place."

"I was coming in the back…saw you and…"

"Oh Greg, I'm sorry," Beth said as soon as she realized what had happened, how panicked he must have been to get Connie's note saying Amanda was home and then drive up to a dark house. "You must have been so worried. I should have thought to at least leave a light burning."

Lightning flashed and Greg turned to catch Amanda, expecting her to propel herself across the room and bury her face in his side.

"Whoa!" she shouted. She had returned to her sewing and as she stitched, she narrated the storm as if she were a color commentator for some sports event. "One of the angels stole the ball. She's headed downfield. Here comes the other team." The thunder rolled. "Go-o-al!" she shouted pumping one fist high in the air and laughing with delight.

Greg looked from his daughter to Beth and back again.

"Beth told me she used to be afraid of thunderstorms, too, but then her daddy told her that it was nothing but God's angels playing some sport. Today Beth and me decided it was soccer."

"I see," Greg replied but the look he gave Beth stated clearly that he didn't get it at all.

"Every time the thunder rolls Amanda decided that the opposing team had stolen the ball and was headed down field. Lightning is, of course, a..." She motioned that Greg should finish the thought.

"Goal?"

"Not like that, Dad. Beth says the professional announcers say, 'Go-o-al!' real loud and drawn out."

Greg picked his daughter up and started to tickle her. "And do the professionals always giggle after they say it?" he teased.

Beth watched the father and daughter laughing with delight and tried to work around the lump that suddenly seemed permanently lodged in her throat. As was her habit, when she didn't know how else to handle a moment, she started to chatter away as she busied herself with multiple tasks.

"Connie came by on their way to Bozeman and she was going to leave Amanda at home but wanted me to know she was there. I was the one who suggested she stay here. Actually I was really glad to have the company as well as the help. After all, I have these cookies to make for the open house at the school and who was going to lick the bowl for me?''

She shoved a sheet of cookies into the oven and turned to start scooping up a fresh batch. ''I just love raw cookie dough and as it turns out, Amanda does too.''

''Beth said we had to save it for dessert, though. She's making supper for us and then we're going to sit in front of the TV and just pig out, isn't that right, Beth?''

Beth glanced at Greg to see how he was taking all of this. ''Well, yeah, that was the deal if a certain young lady finished all her regular food.''

''Sounds like a party,'' Greg said but his voice was quiet and his eyes were on Beth.

''You're invited, Dad, isn't he, Beth?'' Amanda looked at Beth and locked her hands around her father's neck as he held her high in his arms.

''Am I?'' he asked Beth.

Do you want to be? ''Of course. The more the merrier.'' Beth busied herself by checking on the cookies, stirring the pot of chili she'd been heating for their supper and gathering the makings for a mixed salad from the refrigerator. ''I hope this is okay,'' she said. ''It's just leftovers.''

''With a side of raw cookie dough, I'd say it's pretty near perfect,'' Greg replied as his eyes met hers. He set Amanda back on the stool next to her sewing and cleared his throat. "How can I help?"

"Oh heavens, no. You've already put in a full day, not to mention the fact we probably scared you to death not knowing where to find Amanda. You must be exhausted." She saw that she had come very close to the truth and paused in her frenzied activity to really look at him. He was bone weary and had gotten soaked in the storm as he searched for Amanda. "Why don't you go over there next to the woodstove and just relax?"

Greg took her suggestion. He walked across the small room—the bare bones, impersonal room she had somehow managed to make homey and welcoming. He took note of all the many little details that surprised him—things about her surroundings that made him take stock of his preconceived ideas about her.

He sat in the rocker and noticed the way she had padded the seat and back with colorful cushions. The beige carpet was splashed here and there with small braided rugs. He leaned back and watched her working in the small galley kitchen. This was no performance for his benefit. Beth was clearly used to spending time in a kitchen. She was accomplished at juggling the many tasks of putting a meal together and baking cookies at the same time. Occasionally she would lean across the counter and make some comment to Amanda about the sewing project that claimed all of his daughter's attention.

Greg frowned. Beth Baxter was not at all what he

had expected. She was a city girl, used to high-rises and bright lights and—considering her father's money—probably maids, country homes and private schools. Yet, she seemed perfectly at home in these plain surroundings. He glanced away unwilling to let her see how affected he was by her as he watched her work. Closer examination of the small crib quilt Amanda had spread carefully over the small footstool next to the rocker revealed true craftsmanship, a real work of art.

He leaned back in the rocker and noticed a Bible on the table next to the chair, not just any Bible but an old dog-eared, much-used Bible. He picked it up and opened it to the frontispiece. There, in a childlike scrawl similar to Amanda's own ten-year-old hand-writing, were the words: "Presented to Elizabeth Joy Baxter on her tenth birthday. With love and blessings, Grandma Jen."

He closed the Bible and replaced it on the side table. From what he had observed of her in church, he knew that she wasn't faking her deep spiritual roots. It was one more thing that he would never have expected about her. She'd arrived at the park like some drifter out of the night. He'd thought of her as an heiress to a fortune, someone out for an adventure. He had never stopped to imagine her as part of a real family—a daughter, a granddaughter learning to quilt at her grandmother's knee.

Over the past few weeks as his fascination with her had grown in spite of his determination to fight it, the one thing he had used to console himself was that she was just here—on a lark. He'd convinced himself of that and it had kept him from giving in to his curiosity about her. Yet there was something so permanent about the way she had decorated this place, something about her insistence on surrounding herself with mementos and treasures that were well-used and loved, something about the way she obviously valued the ordinary things in life that spoke volumes.

"Impossible," he muttered as a reminder to himself as he once again felt the now familiar draw to her. *She still clings to the idea that there's some master puppeteer up there pulling everybody's strings. We have nothing in common—nothing,* he reminded himself, firmly making it almost a mantra to help get him through the rest of the evening.

"Soup's on," she called gaily and Amanda scrambled to help her bring the food to the small table near the woodstove.

"We should say grace," Amanda announced once she had settled herself in a chair across from her doll. "We used to say grace at every meal before Mom died," she told Beth. "I miss it," she continued matter-of-factly and glanced at her father to see how this little speech was being received.

"Amanda," Greg began.

"I think grace is a terrific idea," Beth interrupted what sounded like it might be the beginning of a reprimand. "Will you do the honors, Amanda?"

Amanda and Beth both folded their hands in prayer and bowed their heads. Amanda waited. "Dad," she said in a stage whisper, "we're waiting. God's waiting."

Greg had no choice. He folded his hands and bowed his head staring at the steaming bowl of chili in front of him.

"God is great. God is good. Thank you, God, for this food," Amanda said softly.

"Amen," Beth chorused with her. Greg added a grudging "Amen."

The food was flavorful and hearty. On top of everything else, the woman could cook. Greg frowned as he helped himself to seconds on the chili.

"Too spicy?" Beth asked. "You're frowning," she added when he gave her a puzzled look.

"No. Just some passing thought," he replied.

"Da-a-d, this is supper time and we don't think about work at mealtime, do we?" Amanda lectured wagging a finger at her father.

He smiled. "It's an old family tradition," he explained to Beth. "No unpleasant thoughts or worries during meals."

"Mom made that rule," Amanda announced and turned her attention back to her chili.

Beth watched Greg for any sign of pain or grief. Instead he smiled at Amanda. "That's right," he said.

"Mom had a lot of rules like that," Amanda continued. "I mean, she wasn't bossy or anything. She'd tell us that the rules were for our own good. What was it she used to say, Dad?"

"That her rules were intended to help us appreciate

what we had while we had it," he answered and his expression and voice both softened as he repeated the words.

"Yeah. I think they were pretty good rules," Amanda declared as she gobbled down the last spoonful of her chili. "I've cleaned my plate. Can we eat cookie dough now?"

"One spoon," Beth agreed. "You don't want to make yourself sick."

"One spoon and two real cookies," Amanda negotiated.

"One cookie," Greg instructed, "and stop trying to con your teacher."

Amanda giggled and very carefully filled a teaspoon to the max with raw cookie dough, then took a long moment to select the largest possible cookie. "Is it okay if me and Trudy watch TV?"

"Trudy and I," Beth corrected. "Would you rather watch a video?"

"Cool."

Beth got the tape loaded into the VCR and gave Amanda the remote. When she turned back to the kitchen, Greg was watching her, his expression unreadable.

"You're thinking again," she said lightly as she began clearing away the dishes.

He got up to help her. "I want to thank you for taking care of Amanda today. I'm sure you discovered that she's terrified of storms and yet you seem to have disarmed that fear completely."

Beth laughed. "The truth is, *I'm* terrified of storms

so I did what was necessary to get us both through the afternoon. I was never so glad to see anyone in my life as I was to see you standing outside my kitchen window.'' The words were out before she could stop them. Afraid that they sounded too forward she quickly added, ''Even if you did scare me half to death.''

He smiled a charming shy smile that was at odds with his usual stern and serious demeanor. ''Sorry about that. I guess I did come off as something of a Peeping Tom.'' He picked up a dish towel and waited for her to wash the first dish so he could dry. ''It's true that I was a little concerned when I read Connie's note about Amanda being home and then saw that our half of the house was dark,'' he admitted.

Beth was surprised that he would openly admit such a thing. He must have been truly upset. She chastised herself for not making sure she left word in other places about Amanda staying with her. ''I should have called somebody. The least I could have done was driven over to Connie's and added to her note. I'm really sorry.'' She handed him a plate and their fingers brushed.

''It's okay,'' he said but he was looking at her hand and she became aware of how close they were standing in the small kitchen. She could actually feel the warmth of him next to her, could smell the scent of his uniform, now rumpled from a day in the field, was aware of the steady solid rise and fall of his chest with each breath he took.

She turned back to the sink, her eyes downcast as

she wondered if there was any possibility that he felt an attraction for her on any level. She tried to think of a topic of conversation that might lighten the moment. He rescued her by mentioning the quilt.

"I don't know much about these things, but that must have taken a lot of patience," he said after complimenting her on its beauty.

They were on safe ground. She could breathe again. She smiled. "My grandmother is the real artist in our family. She still checks my work to be sure the stitches are even and I haven't taken any shortcuts."

"Sounds like a tough lady. How old is she?"

"Eighty-five. She called last night to remind me that my friend's baby is due any time now. And, she added that since I had done this fool thing of running off to the Wild Wild West, I had better get this quilt on the next stage out of here if it was going to be there in time for the baby's arrival. She's a real character."

Greg smiled. "I'd like to meet her sometime."

It was a perfectly innocent statement so why did Beth's heart leap with pleasure? "Are your parents and grandparents still living?" she asked.

"Yep. All of them. Mom and Dad retired from the park service about two years ago and moved to Arizona. My maternal grandparents live there as well. My dad's parents are up in northern Montana."

"How wonderful for Amanda to have all of those generations in her life."

"It's been pretty important. And, of course, Lu's family has been around as well—fewer of them. Lu's mom also died of cancer when Lu was a teenager. We knew the history and thought we were keeping a watch on things but..." His voice trailed off and he got a faraway look in his eyes as he stared out the window into the black night.

Beth swallowed hard. "I know this really is none of my business, Greg, but Amanda..."

His attention was instantly back on her, his dark eyes probing hers. "What about Amanda?"

"It's just that this afternoon while I was helping her with her quilt, Lu's name kept coming up and there was a moment when...I got a feeling that she's concerned, maybe even feeling a little guilty."

His hands clenched the dish towel, his knuckles turning white with the obvious effort to maintain his calm. "Guilty?"

Beth swallowed and plunged on. "She told me that sometimes she can't remember what her mother looked like and that at times like that she has to look at old photographs. It bothers her that she can't always recall the sound of her mother's voice. I think that may be one reason why she quotes her mother so much.

"She talks about her a lot at school as well," Beth added when they had sat in silence for a moment.

This time there was no doubt about the pain that she saw cross his face. She would have done almost anything to spare him that, but he needed to know.

She placed her hand on his. "Greg, I know this is hard for you."

For the first time since she'd met him, he seemed

at a loss. "I know she thinks about Lu a lot. I try to talk to her, answer her questions…" His voice trailed off. "It's just hard because I keep thinking that the real question she must want to ask is *why*."

Beth didn't know what to say. Was he really saying that he was the one still asking why?

"Back in Chicago, there were two occasions when I had to deal with children who lost a parent," Beth said.

He looked at her with surprise and respect. "Really?"

She nodded. "One boy's father was killed in a robbery as he was leaving his office late one night. The other was a boy whose mother died in a car accident right after she and his father had separated."

"That's awful," Greg said.

Beth nodded. "Yeah. In both cases they were there one minute and gone like that." She snapped her fingers.

Greg glanced at Amanda whose attention was riveted on the movie.

"At least with Lu, we had some time—Lu was able to talk to Amanda, help her through it."

Beth nodded. She sensed that she had given him a new insight into his wife's death by telling him about the others. She decided to push her luck.

"I do have a suggestion—something we used with these children in Chicago," she said softly.

Once again she had his full attention, but this time his eyes were filled with pleading.

Help me.

She knew what it would cost a man like Greg to admit that he could manage a huge national park but he could not find the answer to relieving his child's emotional pain.

"We would help the child make a memory book," she continued as if this were a normal conversation in which he was holding up his end of things.

"A memory book," he repeated.

Beth nodded and removed the towel from his hands, draping it over the side of the sink to dry and then starting to put cookie dough onto a clean cookie sheet for baking.

"It works best if you and Amanda work on it together. You let Amanda tell a story—a memory— about her mother or your life as a family when Lu was still alive."

"I can do that," he said more to himself than to her.

"You help her find pictures of Lu and herself and you to illustrate the story."

"We have albums," he said. "Lu spent a lot of time putting them together before…"

Beth swallowed. It hurt to see how hard it was for him to talk about this.

"You can also let Amanda draw pictures as you write the story down—or help her do that. Then you put the whole thing into a scrapbook."

She handed him a freshly baked cookie, which he ate in two bites as he considered the idea.

"Sounds like a big undertaking."

"It doesn't have to be. In fact it works better if you do it a little at a time—over time."

"I don't know. Stirring up all those memories..."

She wanted to ask him if he was afraid of his own pain or causing pain for Amanda.

"I've seen it work," she said casually not wanting to insist. "Basically, you just keep repeating that simple exercise until the book is full or until Amanda is satisfied with the outcome. It does help," she assured him.

Greg watched her turn to put the last pan of cookies into the oven. He was as close as he had ever been to confiding in someone the horrors of his own jumbled feelings related to his wife's death. His anger. His pain. His loneliness. His own guilt. *Pull yourself together, man. It's the storm and the scent of freshly baked cookies and this woman mothering your child that you're reacting to. Get a grip.*

"It's an interesting idea. Maybe we'll talk about it—Amanda and me."

He did a little drum rhythm on the counter with the flat of his hands and stood. "Well, it's late." He offered Beth a handshake. "Thanks again for everything."

She looked at his outstretched hand and deliberately took hold of it as if they were holding hands instead of shaking hands. She turned a formal thank-you into something else—something friendlier and more intimate.

"Any time," she murmured as she squeezed his

hand and released it. She crossed in front of him to gather Amanda's things in her backpack.

Greg watched Beth kneel to pick up the scraps of fabric and the crudely sewn quilt Amanda had started. She carefully pressed the creases from it with her flat palms and he recalled how those gentle, long-fingered hands had felt touching his. He heard Amanda sniffling back tears.

"I'll never understand how you can watch that movie a dozen times and still cry every time," he teased, glad to have something other than Beth to focus on.

"It's a girl thing, Dad," Amanda said as she shrugged into her jacket and then put her arms around Beth and gave her a big hug. "I had a lot of fun today. Thanks for making up the story about the storm. I wasn't quite as scared as usual," she added with a whisper.

Beth hugged her back and kissed her on the forehead. "It was all my pleasure. You work on that quilt now and if you need help or more fabric just stop by, okay?"

Amanda beamed. "Sure."

Beth stood up and handed Amanda's backpack to Greg. "That offer goes for you as well, Chief Ranger," she said lightly.

"I don't do much quilting," he said and smiled.

"Pity," she replied and he realized that they were flirting and that it felt pretty normal and nice.

Back in his own place, Greg put Amanda to bed and then sat down at his desk to do some work.

A memory book, Beth had called it. He opened the bottom drawer of the desk and took out a photograph album.

It was one of the ones Lu had put together, one she had been almost desperate to finish. He remembered how she had wanted him to work on it with her, and how he had refused. After her death, he had put it away.

In those days the pain of looking at her laughing healthy face and remembering all the good times they had shared had been more than he could bear. As time went on he had thought about the album less and less—until tonight. Beth's words rang as true for him as they did for Amanda.

"Amanda is afraid that she's forgetting her mother," Beth had told him.

As he paged through the album he realized that his own mental image of his wife was fading. He also struggled to recall the sound of her voice, the smell of her cologne. The woman who looked back at him from the pages of the album seemed in her glowing health and beauty to be trying to remind him of something important.

"What was that quote you always used to repeat?" He murmured as he stroked the photograph. "You never knew where it came from but it was your favorite."

For an instant the laughing face seemed alive and he heard her voice clearly. "'Life is what happens while we're making other plans,'" he chanted in unison with the words heard only in his mind.

Then the memory changed. The laughter and soft voice that he heard was Beth's. He thought about her talking to Amanda as they made the cookies and worked on the doll quilt. He thought about how she had laughed at the thunderstorm, and gotten Amanda to do the same. He stared at the photograph again.

"I know what you're up to," he said aloud, "but trust me, she's not the right one."

As if Lu were there debating the point, he added, "Maybe it is time to get on with my life, but not with her."

He paused and turned the pages. "No," he continued as if arguing with the woman in the photographs. "I can't take the chance that Amanda will love her and then she'll leave. You of all people should understand that, Lu," he instructed.

Suddenly he recalled the tiny frown lines that used to furrow her brow when Lu didn't agree with him. It was an image as clear as if he had seen her yesterday.

"I know you don't agree, but this time you're just going to have to trust me," he said firmly and closed the album.

Instead of storing it back in the drawer, he left it on the table with all the framed family photographs. Lu looked up at him from a photo of the three of them taken at Yellowstone Lake.

"Okay, I'll admit that the memory book idea isn't half bad. Maybe I'll talk to Amanda about that this week, okay?" He had just done exactly what he'd always done in the face of those challenging little furrows in Lu's brow. He had offered a compromise.

"Dad?"

Amanda stood at the top of the stairs. Her voice was thick with sleep. "Who're you talking to?"

"Myself," he replied. "Go back to bed, kiddo."

He listened for the sound of his daughter's bare feet retracing her steps to her room.

"I've been working way too hard," he muttered as he switched off the light and headed upstairs to tuck her in for the night.

Chapter Seven

The week following the storm passed in a flurry of activity. The children were quite excited about the upcoming open house at the school and kept coming up with new ideas for decorating their classrooms and entertaining their guests. In the face of their enthusiasm the faculty found it hard to say no to anything within reason that they proposed and as a result found themselves spending a lot of extra time at the school helping the children implement their ideas. The other teachers told Beth that they'd never seen the children get so involved in the open house before.

"Are you moving out of the duplex and planning to just live here?" Greg stood at the door of the classroom.

She hadn't heard him come in, but she was inordinately glad to see him.

"It might be easier," she admitted as she leaned

back in her chair and stretched her stiff muscles. "There are just so many things the children want to show their parents and friends. It seems a shame not to try to make that happen when they are so very enthusiastic."

"Not like your students in Chicago?" he asked easing into the room and looking around at the various displays.

Beth laughed. "Heavens no. They would be bored silly with the idea of an old-fashioned open house." She paused. "That's not fair. My students in Chicago were good kids. I was the one who was out of sorts," she admitted.

"Really?" Greg studied her. "I find it hard to believe that you could ever be anything but effervescent."

Beth laughed. "Heavens, you haven't seen me at my worst yet. Trust me, I can be a real pain."

"So why were you out of sorts in Chicago?"

She shrugged. "I'm not sure. As I've told you, I had—have a wonderful life there. A fulfilling career in teaching and a full social life. My family is the best."

"But?"

"But I wanted something more," she admitted. "Doesn't that sound extraordinarily selfish?"

"Not really. Depends on what more you wanted? Money? Fame?"

She laughed. "I think those are two of the things I was running away from."

"Aha. So, when you said on that first night that

you hadn't come here on the run, you weren't being entirely truthful.''

Beth blushed. ''I didn't mean it that way. Just that sometimes being wealthy can be…difficult.''

He raised one eyebrow.

She laughed. ''Yeah, well you know, poor little rich girl and all of that. How on earth did we get off on this?''

''You started it.''

''Lucky you to be the one in the line of fire when I do,'' she joked.

He smiled. ''It's nice to see that it makes you as uncomfortable as my talking about myself makes me.''

''Touché. Anyway, getting back to the topic at hand—the open house. It's a lot of work, but also a lot of fun and the children are really excited about it.''

''But, it's not only the kids who are caught up in this thing,'' he mused.

''All right. I'll admit that I've kind of gone a teensy bit overboard, but the kids are so appreciative of everything and that part is also different from the students in Chicago. They tend to take things like this for granted.''

She watched him as he continued his tour of the room. ''I could turn the tables, you know.''

He glanced at her. ''How so?''

''It appears to me that you've been spending quite a bit of time at your work these past several weeks.

I thought things were supposed to ease up once the high tourist season ended.''

He smiled. ''Guilty,'' he admitted softly. He leaned against the side of her desk. ''How's Amanda doing?''

''What a question! She's your daughter to the core—an overachiever, a born leader and smart as a whip.''

He could not hide his pleasure at her praise. ''She takes after her mother.''

''Some, probably,'' Beth said, ''but I see a lot of you in her, as well. You're a very good parent, Greg.''

''Thanks.''

There was a moment when neither of them seemed to know what to say.

''Are you about ready to head for home?'' he asked finally.

Unable to find her voice, Beth nodded.

''Good. Me, too.''

As they crossed the compound together, he told her about his day. ''The northeast pass has been closed all week.''

''Why?''

''All that rain we got turned to snow in the high elevations.''

''It just seems too early for winter.''

He laughed. ''I thought you Chicago natives were used to cold weather.''

''Well, sure—in January,'' she replied. ''You know *winter?* October—that's autumn.''

"Winter comes a little earlier around here, and speaking of that, you need to be aware of the particular cautions you'll need to take—"

"Oh, please not another lecture," she begged.

"Just a short one," he assured her and then proceeded to list all the measures she needed to take before heading out into the park for the next several months.

Beth sighed. He just couldn't help himself, she decided. He really should have been a teacher.

In spite of his growing attraction for the woman, Greg was determined to maintain a purely friendship-based relationship with Beth. He didn't want to offend her or upset Amanda, but he was convinced that spending too much time—especially time alone—with Beth would only increase his fascination with her and no good could possibly come of that.

On Saturday, he was finishing up some end of the season reports when he heard the familiar sound of Beth's distinctive laughter outside his office window. He glanced out and saw her talking to a couple of the park's naturalists. She'd certainly made a place for herself among the staff in the short time she'd been there. They accepted her as one of their own, sought her out to join them in various activities and brought up her name in casual conversation with disconcerting regularity.

She was outfitted for a serious hike complete with water bottle, backpack and walking stick and he strained to hear bits and pieces of the conversation.

"...science unit on trees," he heard her say. "I'm off to collect samples." She waved and headed toward one of the main trailheads.

Greg forced his concentration back to his paperwork. Beth couldn't get into trouble collecting a bunch of leaves. There were at least a couple dozen different trees along the trail she had chosen. She should have all the samples she needed within an hour.

But by late afternoon she had not returned. Greg had watched for her. Thinking he might have missed her or that she might have come back into town another way, he walked over to the duplex.

Amanda was working on her quilt.

"Has Miss Baxter come home?" He asked and hoped it sounded like a normal casual question.

"Nope, but don't worry, Dad. Beth will find her way home. She's really good at maps."

The trouble was, Greg hadn't seen a map in her hand. She'd hiked the trail before—or part of it, but it would be easy to get distracted and make a wrong turn.

"I have to go out on the trail for a bit," he said. "I should be back by six, okay?"

"Sure, Dad."

"Okay, see you later," Greg said and headed across the compound and up the trail he had seen Beth take several hours earlier.

It was one of those days that seem scripted by some Hollywood director. The sky was a cloudless blue, the air sharp and crisp with a hint of cold weather to come. The brilliant golden leaves of the aspens rustled in the October breeze. But Greg Stone knew that a day like this could be distracting for the novice hiker. It was a day when tourists would stop in the middle of the path and inhale deeply, then trudge on deeper and deeper into the park, anxious to discover untold beauty just beyond the next bend or rise.

Even if she had brought a map and paid attention to the markings along the trail Beth could have gotten turned around, think she was headed back toward town and actually be moving farther away with every step. Or knowing Beth, she could know exactly where she was but not care that she was moving away from town.

She always seemed to be going in ten different directions as she juggled the routine schooling of the children, plans for the open house at the school and maintained contact with family members and friends back in Chicago. On top of that, it seemed to Greg that her acceptance by the rest of the teachers and park staff had gotten her involved in all sorts of extra activities—church things plus the book discussion group and a bike-hike club.

Greg picked up the pace, oblivious now to the scenery as he focused on one thing—finding her before dark. He could hear the rush of the waterfall as he climbed the path. His breath was coming in bursts of exertion now and he lengthened his stride to conquer the steep slope of the trail. The water crashed over rocks and dropped twenty-five feet straight down to a pool on the other side. It wasn't the highest waterfall in the park but to a novice caught in its drop, it could be maiming or even deadly.

Greg stood at the summit and looked down, afraid of what he might find on the great flat rocks at the base of the falls.

She was there all right, standing on a large rock in the middle of the gurgling water and quite some distance downstream from the falls. She was gesturing with her hands as if conducting an orchestra or having an animated conversation with someone. Greg half slid and half stumbled down the steep trail. When he reached the base, he moved through the trees and underbrush toward the stream.

"Okay, you can go now," Beth shouted.

Greg paused knowing there was no way she could know he was there since he was coming up on her from behind and the noise of the falls drowned out any sounds he might make.

"Shoo," she said and made the same flinging gesture with her hands that she had used equally as ineffectively with the bear that first night. Then she placed both hands on her hips and faced her adversary.

Greg lifted the branch of a low cedar. All the while his brain raced as he tried to figure out what he would do to rescue her from a bear once again. This time he didn't have a stun gun handy. He searched the shoreline for the source of her dismay.

A large bull elk stood at the edge of the stream staring directly at Beth. Greg grinned.

"Now look," Beth shouted at the elk above the

noise of the falls. "I've about had it with you. I really don't need this in my life right now. I've got problems of my own, and I'm not the least bit interested in stealing your harem or joining it. So go away."

The elk did not move. He was still exactly between her and where she needed to go to get back on the trail to town. "You know, Chief Ranger Stone is not going to be happy about having to comb the woods for me after dark. You know how he gets when we don't follow the rules," she added.

Greg bristled and waited.

"Come on, Mr. Elk, give me a break. The guy already thinks that I redefine the word *tenderfoot*. If I don't head back now, it's going to get dark."

The elk rolled his head and appeared to look at the sun low in the western sky.

"That happens you know, like clockwork every day. Sun comes up. Sun goes down." She was squatting now, her hands dangling between her knees as she continued to observe the elk. "Tell you what," she said and stood up. "Why don't I just mosey on over to this next rock…" She hopped one rock closer to the shore. The elk eyed her.

"You see, I really didn't mean to disturb you. I just wanted to get a leaf from that tree there. I teach the children, you know."

The elk made a low sound and bent to take a drink of water.

"Well, maybe it's not as glamorous as being the king of the bull elks but I like it," she said defensively. "And frankly, I'm quite good at it no matter what Chief Ranger Stone might think."

She eased herself onto the next rock. The elk was instantly on alert. "He's not a bad sort—the Chief Ranger," she said as she continued to slowly work her way across the rocks toward the shore. "He's actually quite interesting if you like the stubborn type."

Interesting? Greg took some offense at that. He had been called handsome and attractive and even a hunk and all she could come up with was *interesting?*

"He has this adorable daughter—Amanda? Have you met her? No? Well, she's really special." She was almost to shore and the elk was still watching her but hadn't moved. "Well, it's been a real treat chatting with you, Mr. Elk, but I think I may hear your wife…or harem or whatever calling you for supper." The elk took two steps along the shore in her direction.

"No," she shouted.

The elk froze.

"Look, I'm tired and hungry and I want to go home. I've really bent over backward here, and you're beginning to remind me more and more of our obstinate Chief Ranger. It wouldn't kill you to just turn around and leave. You can come back in five minutes and I promise you, I won't be anywhere near here. Deal?"

The elk gave a snort.

Greg smiled in spite of himself. What was it about this woman that made him want to laugh with delight? Why on earth hadn't he let her know he was standing not ten feet from her? Because he wanted to watch her and listen to her ridiculous patter. Quickly and stealthily he moved back up the trail. Halfway up the waterfall, he stopped and cupped his hands to his mouth and called her name. "Beth. Beth Baxter. Are you out there?"

"Greg?" She sounded relieved.

Greg smiled and felt enormously pleased with himself.

"Down here," she shouted and waved her arms wildly.

Greg acknowledged her wave and chuckled at the way he had fooled her as he retraced his steps down the path to the edge of the stream. "What are you doing out there in the middle of the stream?" he asked gruffly as he held out his hand to help her step from the last rock to the shore.

"There was this humongous bull elk," she said breathlessly. "I was right over there collecting leaves and all of a sudden he comes crashing through the trees and he had this awesome rack and he's doing that bugle thing they do when they think there's somebody trying to steal their women and—"

"I don't see an elk," Greg said pretending to look around. "Oh, you mean that guy way over there?"

"Trust me, five minutes ago, he was right here. Maybe your shouting drove him away."

"If that was the case, why didn't you shout at him?" They had started back up the trail.

"I did," she protested.

No, you carried on a normal conversation with the beast, he thought and grinned.

"Are you laughing at me?" she demanded glancing back in time to see him smile.

"No ma'am."

She continued to climb the steep trail. He tried not to notice how she was equally attractive from behind as she was face-to-face. He tried to think about something else and instead found himself wondering what it might be like to kiss her.

As they reached the top of the falls, she stopped to catch her breath. "He was enormous," she protested as she plopped down in the high grass to adjust her hiking boot.

"I believe you," he assured her. "The elk can be a most *interesting* not to mention *stubborn* beast."

She gave him a strange look and he noticed the color in her cheeks, which he was pretty sure, was new and had nothing to do with the exertion of the climb. He liked having her be the one unsure of what was happening for once.

He knelt and helped her with the knots in the wet laces of her boots. His fingers shook slightly, and he cast about for anything resembling a safe topic of conversation.

"By the way," he said, "I want to thank you for the memory book idea."

"You're welcome. Is it working?"

"There's one problem."

"What?" It was unnerving the way she focused every ounce of her concentration on him.

"Well, I'm still not really sure how to go about it. I mean, I gathered up all the pictures and some letters and drawings Lu made, but after that I'm afraid I'm lost and you know how smart Amanda is. If I try to do this and mess it up, she'll see right through me and wonder what's really going on."

"But gathering all of those things is a wonderful way to begin," Beth praised him.

"Maybe," Greg replied but he sounded anything but sure. "Look, I was wondering if you might be willing to work on it with Amanda. I mean, coming from me she might view it as something she needs to do for me. I thought about what you said, and I agree that it's really important for her to focus on her own memories, not try to help me handle mine."

Beth's expression softened. "Of course," she said and he was pretty sure that tears brimmed. "I'm really touched that you would trust me to help Amanda with something so personal."

"Yeah, well…"

What on earth was happening here? He had never wanted to kiss a woman as much in his life. He stood and offered her a hand up from her reclining position.

"Come on," he said. "We need to make time if we're going to get home before dark."

Beth accepted his hand and peppered him with questions about photos and other sources of materials for Amanda's memory book. As they made their way along the trail it seemed perfectly natural to continue holding hands as the brilliant gold leaves of the aspens fluttered like butterflies around them.

Chapter Eight

~

Greg lay in bed and watched the slow arrival of dawn. He hadn't had a lot of sleep. In fact he'd noticed that ever since Beth Baxter's arrival in the park, sleep had been in short supply for him.

He considered their encounter at the waterfall and the hike back to town. By the simple act of taking her hand and not letting go, he had changed everything. No longer could he pretend to ignore the way his heart tripped every time he saw her walking across the compound or heard her laughter. No longer could he dismiss the fact that he was always watching for her, watching *out* for her. No longer could he postpone dealing with the fact that he was attracted to her in a way that went beyond mere interest or casual friendship.

"Morning, Dad." Amanda plopped herself onto the foot of his bed.

"Morning, kiddo."

"Are we going to church today?"

"Sure."

"Do you think Beth will be there?"

She always was. She always sat in the third row right where he could see her clearly as he sat in the choir.

"Probably so."

Amanda pulled one of his pillows around and lay down. "I like her—Miss Baxter," she said as she studied the ceiling. "I didn't think I was going to and then I did. Funny, huh?"

"That's the way things go sometimes," Greg replied but his mind was on Beth.

"She always looks so pretty, especially when she's in church, don't you think so, Dad?"

Greg grabbed Amanda and began tickling her. "I think that if a certain young lady doesn't get back to her room and start dressing, we're going to be late."

Amanda giggled and broke away from him. "I'm going," she said, still laughing. "Hey, Dad, how about pancakes?" she called.

He got up and made her pancakes, and continued to think about Beth. He couldn't get the woman out of his mind.

Of course, any idea of an actual romance between them was destined to be heartbreak for somebody. Beth was strong-willed. She was also a firm believer, and that was the real problem.

She would only tolerate his nonbelief for so long before trying to change him. That would lead to arguments. Then she would leave. And what of Amanda, getting more and more attached to her? If he did anything that might encourage Amanda's obvious hope that something might develop between them, Amanda was bound to end up brokenhearted.

Weeks earlier when Beth had surprised him with her quiet perception and understanding of his point of view at the book discussion group, he had permitted himself to consider the possibility of getting to know her a little better.

That night in her place when she had baked cookies and cared for his daughter, comforting her when he wasn't there to do it, he had settled on friendship as the best course. He needed to stick with that. Good-buddy-no-strings friendship. That was the ticket.

He poured batter in nearly perfect circles in the hot skillet and smiled.

The woman had certainly gotten herself in a fix yesterday with that elk. By the time they'd hiked back to town it had been dark, but he'd barely noticed the long hike. Talking to her was getting easier every time they were together. He liked showing off the park to her, liked her curiosity and liked having the answers to impress her.

He frowned as he flipped the pancakes. On the other hand, what if he hadn't come along? She'd still be out there—scared and cold or perhaps worse, injured or maimed. He shuddered. For all her adjustment to the ways of park life, she was still a tenderfoot.

The way he saw it, he had two choices. As her

friend, he could either let things take their course and worry himself to death whenever she took a notion to go off on her own, or he could make sure she knew the ropes. Number two was clearly the better choice. If he had confidence that she had been properly instructed, he could relax and stop watching for her every second.

He served up pancakes on a plate and set them in the oven to stay warm.

"Amanda? Breakfast," he called up the stairs as he filled two mugs with coffee and rummaged through his desk for the things he needed. "I have to go next door for a few minutes, okay?"

He gathered his maps and his thoughts. There was nothing to be gained by permitting himself to give in to the sort of romantic attraction signaled by that innocent bit of hand-holding. Even if she were willing to accept him for the nonbeliever that he was, he couldn't very well give up his job or his life in the park to follow her to Chicago. It was simply impractical to think anything could come of a romance between the two of them. And the one thing Greg Stone knew for certain about himself was that he was a very practical man.

Beth had never been much of a morning person. Especially on the weekends, she liked the opportunity to ease into the day, savoring such time-honored rituals as lingering over coffee and the paper and lounging about in her pajamas until time to get ready for church. This particular Sunday she planned to indulge herself to the fullest.

Her adventure of the day before had left her exhausted with aches in muscles she hadn't even thought existed. She hated to miss church, but this was one morning when she definitely needed to heed God's command that there be a day of rest.

She stretched out on the sofa and closed her eyes then immediately opened them. It was useless. She hadn't been able to get back to sleep since she had first wakened at dawn thinking about Greg Stone—about the way his large tanned hand had engulfed hers, about how being with him seemed more and more the right thing for her. She thought about his laughter and the serious expression that crossed his face whenever he was worried about something. She thought about what a wonderful father he was to Amanda. She thought about the times the three of them had shared—times when they had almost seemed like a family.

She sighed and pulled her knees to her chest in an effort to relieve her aching back. Who was she kidding? Wasn't it obvious that Greg Stone was still mourning his wife? To hear Connie and the others talk, the woman had been about as close to a saint as they come. And he had certainly made it crystal clear that he wasn't interested in getting involved—especially with her.

On top of that, she had to admit that his determination to turn his back on the very faith that could have sustained him through all of this was a problem for her. Beth believed firmly in the necessity of a strong spiritual foundation to see a person through life. Certainly strong shared spiritual values were the basis of any successful relationship. Under other circumstances she and Greg might have had a chance. But Beth had witnessed far too many situations where people went into a relationship thinking they would change each other, and she knew that she wouldn't be able to keep herself from trying to change Greg Stone—to bring him back to his faith.

"Argh-h-h!" she cried aloud in her best imitation of a comic strip character's woeful cry.

There was a hesitant knock on the door, followed by the unmistakable bass of Greg's voice. "Beth?"

Beth glanced down at her rumpled flannel pajamas. She knew they probably were more presentable than her uncombed hair. She cleared her throat to get the sleep out of it. "Coming," she said cheerfully. She winced as she rolled off the couch, hastily ran her fingers through her hair and struggled into her robe.

"Hi. You're up and out early," she said as she opened the door and leaned on it for support as pain shot through her lower back.

"Can I come in?" He held up the mugs of coffee and she saw that he was trying hard to balance them plus a bunch of papers he held clutched under one arm.

"Sure." She swung the door wide and stepped aside to let him pass.

He headed straight for her kitchen table, handed her one mug of coffee and set the other one on the counter. "Cream, no sugar, right?" he said as he turned his attention to arranging the various documents he had brought with him.

"Right," she replied as she cradled the mug to warm her hands and peered over his shoulder at the papers. "What's all this?"

"These are topographical maps of every trail in the park. We don't need to go through each and every one of them today, but we should at least cover the trails closest to town here. The rest we can get to on an as-needed basis." He paused to take a breath and a gulp of his coffee. "This, for example, is the map for the trail you hiked yesterday. Judging by your stiff movements this morning, I would guess that you were unprepared for its steep climbs."

"I'm still breaking in my hiking boots," she offered weakly.

He glanced at her bare feet and then immediately back to the map. "You should wear them some each day," he advised. "Now then, as you will see, I've highlighted the best route on this particular trail—red is for the short circuit, which is what I would advise for the time being. Once you've gotten a bit more seasoned as a hiker you can tackle the blue and perhaps even the green. You're quite athletic and have clearly had some good training in other sports so it wouldn't surprise me if you could skip directly from red to green."

"Thank you, I think," Beth said dryly. She rubbed sleep from her eyes with the back of one hand and took another sip of the coffee. "You don't mind if I sit for the rest of this lecture, do you Professor?'' She perched on the edge of one of the high bar stools near the counter. "Ah, look at this. I have a topographical view of the *topographical* map. Lovely."

Greg frowned. "This is serious, Beth. You cannot just go wandering off willy-nilly with no objective in mind."

"I have never gone off willy-nilly in my life," she protested. "I don't even know what *willy-nilly* is."

"You dropped everything you had going for you in Chicago and came here to Yellowstone," he said quietly. "That certainly qualifies."

Beth pulled herself to her full height, which still left her several inches shorter than he was. "Well, aren't you the perfect one to lecture someone about life choices? You, of course, have your own life firmly in hand, don't you? That's probably why you're so cheerful all the time."

He scowled down at her. "I'm trying to offer a little friendly help here. Do you understand what could have happened if I hadn't come along yesterday? You could have been out there stumbling around in the dark all night."

"Ha! That's fine advice coming from someone who's been stumbling around in the dark—spiritually speaking—for nearly two years now." *Where had that come from? Why was she getting so upset?* Beth glanced down at her bare toes. "I'm sorry," she said. "That was out of line."

He let out his breath as if he'd been holding it for several minutes. He walked the two paces it took for him to reach the sink and tossed the remains of his coffee down the drain. "I think I know what's going on here," he said.

"Good." Beth let out her own sigh of relief that the tension between them had eased. She smiled. "Maybe you could give me a clue?"

He held out his hand to her and she knew he wasn't offering the formal handshake. Hesitantly, she placed hers in his. "This," he said and his voice was unsteady as he closed his fingers around hers. "This is what's going on."

Beth swallowed hard. "Okay. Should we talk about it?"

He studied their intertwined fingers as if seeking answers. "I'm attracted to you," he admitted.

"But?"

"Beth, you have a life—a real life—out there. You have family and friends and probably an apartment that you've turned into some kind of country home in the midst of the city. You are the daughter of a very prominent man and you have a position in the community—your community." He released her hand reluctantly.

"Come over here and sit down and let me tell you a little something about that perfect life you seem to have assigned to me." She took a step toward the living room and froze.

Greg was immediately at her side. "Beth, what's wrong?"

"I seem to be having a little problem with my

back," she replied and grimaced as a fresh pain shot through her. "I'll be fine. I just need a little rest."

Greg led her gently toward the sofa, removing the back cushions to give her more room. "Lie down," he ordered. "Put these under your knees. A back injury is nothing to take chances with. Why didn't you say something?" He stacked the cushions under her knees and she had to admit that she felt immediate relief. He went upstairs and she could hear him rummaging around in the small bathroom. "There are aspirin in the kitchen," she called.

"Kitchen," he muttered as he hurried back downstairs and toward the galley. "They call it a *medicine cabinet* for a reason," he added under his breath.

"Sorry. I just don't seem to get headaches in the bathroom. The kitchen makes more sense to me."

He rolled his eyes, looking a great deal like his daughter in the action. "Take these." He handed her the pills and held a glass of water to her lips.

She swallowed and made a face. "Yuk."

Greg put the glass aside and pulled the rocker next to the couch. "Okay, tell me the story of little Beth Baxter in Chicago," he said as he settled back, clearly prepared to stay for the long haul.

"You know, it's not all seashells and balloons—being the only child of one of Chicago's most famous couples. Yeah, yeah, I know—poor little me, but believe it or not, it does have its downside."

"Such as?"

"You don't always know who to trust—who your friends are. That may be the worst part."

Her voice had taken on a wistful uncertain tone that surprised him. The one thing he had assumed was that Beth Baxter was always very sure of herself and of those around her. "What else?"

She shrugged. "The usual. It's a pain to be known your whole life as *the only daughter of...* or worse, *the sole heir to the Baxter fortune.*" She actually shuttered with disgust.

"You were a teacher there—you certainly didn't need the work, but you were a teacher."

"I love children. I love watching them learn, being there when the lights go on in their eyes, watching them discover an idea."

"So, why did you leave and come out here? You said yourself that your students there were bright and not so terrible."

She adjusted herself slightly and grimaced at the movement. He resisted the urge to help her. Touching her would not be a good idea at the moment. He was far too attracted to her to risk any contact, and it would shoot holes in his plan to be her friend and nothing more. "I mean, why not just keep on teaching there?"

"In the private school where I taught, the students all come from money and have all the advantages life can give. What they tend to know about the baser realities of life, they've picked up from reading or movies."

"That's natural," Greg said.

"In some ways their lives are actually hampered by their advantages. It can actually stunt curiosity and that can mean that they are less open to the adventures of learning. Not in all cases, of course, but—''

"So you left and came here."

"It's not like I ran out on them," she argued as if he had accused her of something. "They have Evelyn Schuller, after all."

"I didn't say you ran out on anybody."

"It's just that I was getting frustrated and that wasn't doing them or me any good," she continued defensively.

"I see."

"I thought if I took part in the exchange program, it might generate some new ideas in me for how best to reach those students in Chicago and the change in teachers for a year would shake them up a bit, as well. From their letters, I can tell that Evelyn is a hit."

Greg nodded. "How's it working out for you here?"

She smiled. She glowed and he basked in the loveliness of that smile.

"It has been so much more than I expected, so different, so exciting," she gushed. "I mean it, Greg. I never expected to feel such…such a sense of community…."

Her eyes widened as if she'd just made a wonderful discovery.

"That's it," she said more to herself than to him.

"What's it?" he asked.

"It's this place, these people—I feel this incredible sense of belonging, of being accepted for myself in a way I've never truly been able to experience before."

"You make it sound as if your life in Chicago was miserable."

"Oh heavens, no. Don't get me wrong," she rushed to add. "I have a fabulous family—my parents are two of the most down-to-earth people you'd ever want to meet. My grandmother is always reminding us that if the family money isn't used for good then what's the point. We have grand times together and I miss them all terribly, but this place...these people...Connie and Al, Amanda, even you..."

He knew she meant it in a teasing way, but his heart beat in triple time and he had to swallow several times to gain control of his voice. Unable to get a handle on his emotions, he reverted to the safe course. "The exchange program is just that, Beth—a temporary exchange of roles. In a few months you'll head back to Chicago...."

"Maybe I will and maybe I won't," she replied. "I know you don't necessarily believe this but I really think I've been brought here for some purpose beyond just teaching for a year. I haven't yet figured it all out but I have faith that God will show me in His own good time."

If he had needed anything to remind him of the differences between them, she had just delivered it.

"I think you're kidding yourself," he replied with characteristic bluntness. "Even God can't change the fact that you're only here for a short time."

Chapter Nine

"Look, just because your own faith has taken a holiday..." Beth began, frowning. She was working overtime to understand that trying to change him simply wouldn't work. Was it asking too much for him to show a little more respect for her point of view?

She saw that she had hit a nerve. His eyes flashed with irritation, but she couldn't help herself, she kept pushing, asking the questions that she'd wondered about for weeks.

"Tell me, Greg, before Lu died, was your faith strong?"

"What's that got to do with this discussion?"

"Just indulge me—you're questioning the presence of my faith. Why can't I question the absence of yours?"

"All right. Yes, I was a believer."

"And in those times did you never question anything that happened? Wonder why God would permit this or that? Was your life really that perfect and unspoiled?''

''Of course, I questioned things—that's natural.'' He bit off the words and crossed his arms across his body as he figuratively and literally closed himself off from the discussion.

''And in those days when you turned to God for answers, did you get them?''

''I figured things out,'' he argued. ''I may have thought God was leading me but now I know better.''

''What changed?''

He stared at her openmouthed. ''You *know* what changed.''

''Yes, I do,'' she said quietly. ''What changed is that the questions got harder—more personal. What changed was your commitment to digging for the answers even though it was painful.''

This time he turned completely away from her. ''This is not a discussion I want to have with you or anyone else, Beth.''

''Well, that's too bad, because believe me it's a discussion that one day you *will* have with Amanda. Just how long do you expect her to go along maintaining her own faith when the key influence in her life has turned away from his? Don't you think she knows that you're just going through the motions?''

Greg frowned. ''The subject was your mission here in Yellowstone. You have the absurd notion that you might want to stay.''

''There's nothing absurd about it,'' she argued.

"I would remind you that Evelyn Schuller will return at the end of the year, Beth. We can't afford another teacher on staff here. If you've got any notion of staying on…"

He saw the irritation furrow her flawless features. "Ah. Now, I'm the one who is hitting a nerve," he added. "Did it ever occur to you that the lesson you believe you were sent here to learn might just be to appreciate the life that you left back in Chicago?"

She squirmed her way higher onto the pillows in an effort to assert herself. She succeeded in triggering the pain in her lower back.

Greg appeared oblivious to her discomfort as he relentlessly pursued his point. "Have you thought things through, Beth? Life is hard here. It can be boring. The winters are long, and there's not much to keep a person entertained—especially a person who doesn't have a job."

She bristled and grimaced at the jolt of pain that came with the stiffening of her spine. "I'm a grown woman, Greg. I know life here in the park is different from the life I came from, but trust me, I do a fairly good job of amusing myself. Just because I come from money doesn't mean I expect to be pampered and entertained by others."

"I didn't mean it that way." He sat forward, his hands between his knees. "I only meant that sometimes people romanticize life in the park or in any wilderness setting. There's a kernel of the frontier in every American."

"I can tell the difference between reality and romance," she replied stubbornly.

"Maybe, but Lu—" He stopped. *Where had that come from? He had gotten her off talking about Lu and now here he was back at the topic again.*

Beth gave him her full attention. "What about Lu?"

"Nothing." He stood up. "I have to go. Amanda should have left for Sunday school twenty minutes ago."

"Chicken," Beth muttered and stared out the window, refusing to acknowledge him.

"I'm sorry if I upset you, Beth, but the fact is that you..."

She turned back and looked up at him, her eyes flashing with annoyance. "Not another lecture. Could you just try to refrain from offering me advice? Especially when your own personal life is such a mess, okay?"

"My life is fine," he protested.

"Yeah, right. Try finishing this statement. 'But Lu...'"

He stood there staring back at her.

"Can't do it, can you, Mister I've-Got-My-Life-in-Order?" She turned away again.

Greg crossed the room and opened the door. He stopped for a moment with his back still to her. "Lu romanticized life here. She tried hard to be something she wasn't because she knew I loved being here so much. I always told her that someday we'd leave and live like normal people. But I kept postponing that day because I kept earning promotions. I thought that someday I'd be able to give Lu her dream as she'd given me mine. I thought we had time. I was wrong—dead wrong." He left and closed the door without looking back.

Beth made a move to go after him and cried out in pain and frustration as she collapsed back on the couch. "What does that have to do with me?" she said aloud as if he were still in the room. "I'm not your late wife. I'm telling you that I'm beginning to love the park as much as you do. I'm just this close to telling you that I think I love *you*, Chief Ranger Stone." So much for her resolve to not fall in love with any man whose faith was not as strong as her own.

Why him, God? There are a dozen likely souls out there—good, faith-abiding men. Why this one? She closed her eyes against the hot tears that stung and threatened to break free.

Giving in to her tears was definitely not a good idea. Sobbing took a lot of back action and she really wasn't up to that at the moment. Instead, she picked up one of the pillows he'd moved to the floor and threw it at the door. "I don't need you or any other man to make me happy, Greg Stone." On the other hand, he was doing a bang-up job of making her miserable.

Connie stopped by with hot soup for lunch. "Greg told us you were down," she said as she bustled around the kitchen. "Everyone at church this morning was ready to smother you with a steady flow of company but I persuaded them to let me take the first crack at it. So, what's your pleasure? Nonstop visitors bringing you an array of baked goods and home remedies—not to mention advice? Or something less dramatic?''

"Definitely the latter," Beth replied with a grimace as she eased herself into a more comfortable position. "Was Greg at church then?"

"He walked Amanda over for Sunday school, then said he couldn't stay—something about paperwork at the office." Connie handed Beth a mug of steaming chicken noodle soup. "You two have a fight or something?"

"Of course not," Beth protested. "Yes," she admitted when she saw Connie's skepticism. "Is it that obvious?"

Connie laughed. "Honey, our first clue was Greg. The man is as transparent as that windowpane when it comes to you."

"He is also the most exasperating, mule-headed, opinionated..."

"Uh-huh. Eat your soup." Connie perched on the arm of the couch and nibbled a cracker. "The way I see it, the two of you are on a collision course, and yet you keep missing each other. It's the most incredible thing. You like him. He likes you. Amanda adores you both. The Lord indeed works in mysterious ways His wonders to perform but I have to admit that this time, the big fella has me completely stumped."

"It won't work," Beth said miserably. "We're too different."

"No, you're too much alike—both of you trying to be noble and think three steps ahead of what's really happening here. You're missing the moment, honey. Snap out of it. Pay attention."

She polished off the cracker and brushed the crumbs off her lap. "Got to run. Somebody will be by later this afternoon with supper. Try to resist the urge to rearrange the furniture until then, okay?"

"Aye, aye," Beth replied with a mock salute. She watched Connie head for the door. "You really think he likes me?"

"Gee, I don't know. Why don't I pass him a note during study hall and see what he says?" Connie teased. She laughed as she left, ducking the pillow Beth flung in her direction.

Beth was running out of pillows.

"Beth?"

Beth's eyes fluttered open and immediately shut again. It was dark in the room. She must have slept the afternoon away.

"Miss Baxter? Dad and I brought supper." Amanda was kneeling next to the couch. "Dad made turkey sandwiches. I helped."

"That's nice of you, honey. Turn on that light, okay?" Beth blinked at the sudden flare of light in the room. She focused on a tray on the kitchen counter that hadn't been there earlier. "Where's your dad?"

"We forgot the mustard—Dad has this special cranberry mustard he likes on his turkey sandwich. He went to get it." Amanda rushed to straighten the covers as Beth struggled to sit up. "He told me to come on over and wake you up."

"How was Sunday school?" Beth moved gingerly and recorded the fact that she was in decidedly less pain than she had been earlier.

"Pretty good. We did the Good Samaritan lesson today." Amanda grinned. "We're supposed to perform a Good Samaritan act before next Sunday. Do you think this counts?"

"Absolutely," Beth assured her. "Could you get my hairbrush off my dresser?"

"Sure." Amanda took off up the stairs at a run.

"And a pair of socks," Beth called. "In the bureau."

"Okay," Amanda shouted.

The front door opened letting in a gust of the chill night air. Beth looked up at Greg and wondered if there would ever come a time when her heart would react normally to his comings and goings in her life. She didn't think there was much chance of that. "Hi."

"Feeling better?" he asked but instead of coming closer or even making direct eye contact, he headed straight for the counter and began unwrapping the sandwiches and spreading them with mustard.

"Some." *This is going well,* she thought with a sardonic sigh. "Look, I'm sorry about earlier but—"

"Not a biggie," he replied with a dismissive wave of his hand which only served to infuriate her more.

"Beth? Do you want your mirror, too?" Amanda called from the bedroom.

"Sure, honey."

Amanda brought the requested items. "Oh hi, Dad." She made an attempt at fluffing a pillow behind Beth's back. No doubt she had seen the nurses who cared for her mother do the same thing.

Beth pushed herself a little higher on the pillows and risked a glance in the mirror. It was worse than she had imagined. Her hair stood up in funny little spikes where she had slept on it and her left cheek mirrored the pattern of the chenille throw pillow. She quickly brushed her hair and handed the mirror and brush back to Amanda. "Thanks."

"You look pretty even when you don't feel good, doesn't she, Dad?"

Greg glanced up and then back at the sandwiches. "Come pour the milk, Amanda," was all he said.

He brought Beth a plate filled with the sandwich, chips and fresh fruit. Suddenly she was ravenous. "Looks good enough to eat," she quipped and Amanda exploded into laughter.

The sound of childish giggles filling the small close room broke the tension. Greg smiled at his daughter and then at Beth. "Then, let's eat," he said relieving Amanda of one of the glasses of milk she carried in each hand.

After Amanda had led them in thanks, Beth bit into her sandwich. "Amanda tells me they worked on the lesson of the Good Samaritan in Sunday school today,'' she said.

"Yeah, Dad, what have you done today to be a Good Samaritan?"

"He took care of me twice in one day," Beth replied before Greg could answer. She watched him to see what his reaction would be.

"It's my pleasure," he said softly.

"That's very good, Dad," Amanda announced. "Mrs. Clark said the best Good Samaritan is the one who doesn't do it for any reason other than because it's the right thing to do. Then it gives them pleasure even as it helps the poor and downtrodden." Amanda's imitation of the oh-so-proper Mrs. Clark was perfect.

Beth giggled at the same time she tried to take a gulp of her milk and ended up snorting the milk out her nose.

Greg grinned. "Very classy," he observed handing her a napkin.

"You know how classy we high-society Chicago girls are," she teased back and was thrilled to see how his eyes softened as he watched her.

"We have cake," Amanda announced.

"Chocolate?" Beth asked.

"Chocolate-chocolate chip," Amanda confided. "Sara's mom made it for you."

"Only if you eat *all* of your sandwich, young lady," Greg instructed.

"Ah, Dad."

In a thinly veiled attempt to disguise the fact that

she was only pretending to nibble at her sandwich, Amanda kept up a lively conversation relaying to them the latest gossip about each of the students in the school. Beth smiled because what Amanda failed to notice was that by occasionally taking a bite of the sandwich, she was in fact finishing it. She saw that Greg had caught on as well and between the two of them, they peppered Amanda with questions to keep her talking and eating.

"Look at the time," Greg said finally. "Guess we'd better head back home, kiddo. School tomorrow."

Amanda looked stricken. "Dad, the cake, remember?" she said in a stage whisper.

"Oh, yeah." He snapped his fingers and then grinned down at her. "Cake."

Amanda giggled. "I'll take care of everything. You stay here and sit with Beth, okay?"

"Works for me," Greg said, his voice taking on a more serious tone.

For what seemed like the hundredth time since he'd first come through the door early that morning, Beth wished she'd had the good sense to struggle into something slightly more becoming than her flannel pajamas.

"How's the back?" he asked as he sat back down in the rocking chair.

"Much better."

He frowned.

"Truly," she assured him. "I think by morning I should be absolutely fine."

"You could take a day off. Connie can sub for you. She told me to tell you she can pull your kids in with hers—she's done it before."

"I'll keep that in mind. Connie is going to call me first thing tomorrow just to be sure I can hobble over."

He smiled and nodded.

They had run out of things to say, and Amanda seemed to be taking her own sweet time dishing up the cake.

"About earlier..." they said in unison.

"You first," he said.

"I just wanted to say that I didn't mean to snap at you. I know you were just trying to avoid a painful topic, and it wasn't fair of me to keep pressing you." He started to interrupt but she held up her finger indicating she wasn't finished. "What bothered me a lot was the fact that you seem to assume that your wife and I—being women—are somehow dependent on you or some other man for our welfare and happiness. That you must blame yourself for whatever it is you think Lu wanted out of life. My guess is that she had exactly what she wanted—you and Amanda. We each make our own choices in life. Lu did. I do. From everything I've heard about your wife, she was content and happy. She clearly loved you and adored Amanda, and she was a woman of enormous faith. Forgive me for saying it, but I think she would be more disappointed now in the way you've turned away from God than she ever was about living in some house on the hill."

Greg frowned. "Surely you can understand that it's a real stretch for anybody to believe in God when somebody as loveable and young as that little girl ends up without a mother." He spoke through gritted teeth and in a low tone so Amanda wouldn't overhear him.

Beth paused, willing herself to compose her thoughts and choose her words carefully. "Greg, what I understand is that by turning away from God at the very moment when you need His help the most, you put yourself and Amanda in an incomprehensible position—you deprive yourself and your daughter of the very foundation of all hope and comfort." Her voice was low but her tone was intense. "He is there to help you endure these difficult times, not to bring them on you."

To her astonishment, Greg answered her with a wry smile. "I thought you disapproved of people who lectured," he said. He was smiling but his eyes flashed.

"Cake," Amanda announced and both adults put on their best forced smiles for the benefit of the child.

The two of them focused all of the attention on Amanda and as soon as he had consumed the last bite of his cake, Greg stood. "Now, we really do have to go," he said, still not looking directly at Beth. "Miss Baxter needs her rest and tomorrow is a school day, honey."

Amanda kissed Beth's cheek while Greg carried the dishes to the kitchen and rinsed them. "I'm really sorry you hurt your back," she whispered, "but I think Dad likes looking after you."

Beth hugged Amanda. "Thanks for coming," she replied. "I'll see you tomorrow at school."

"Good night," Greg said stiffly from his position near the door. "Call if you need anything during the night."

"Thanks for everything," Beth called. "I'll be fine." She hated this. They needed to finish their conversation. "Greg, I…"

"Good night, Beth." The door closed behind him.

Chapter Ten

A week passed. Then two. The snows were a regular thing now. The northeast entrance to the park was closed for the season. The days turned from golden to gray as the dry leaves crunched underfoot like the wads of paper the children discarded at school.

The seasonal changes weren't the only chilling aspects of life in the park. Ever since that night when Greg and Amanda had brought her supper, Greg had had to work overtime to keep things purely casual with Beth.

"The woman is dangerous," he reminded himself as he stood at his living room window and watched her hurry across the compound on her way to school.

She made him question the things that he thought had gotten him through the terrible months following Lu's death. And most of all, she made him feel hope again.

She acted as if everything was perfectly normal between them whenever they passed on the street or on their way in or out of the neighboring houses.

"Are you completely oblivious to the effect you have on me, Beth Baxter?" he murmured watching her caress the head of one of her students as together they walked into school.

Greg forced himself to move away from the window and to put any thought of Beth Baxter out of his mind. She was the most infuriating, exasperating woman he'd ever known.

On the night of the school's open house, Amanda was nervous and excited. She had been elected by her classmates to act as the narrator for the program.

The room was getting pretty crowded. Just about everybody in town had come. She spotted Beth across the room looking just as pretty as she always did as she greeted each and every person. Amanda liked the way Beth had of taking a person's hand between both of hers. She'd been practicing that in her room, and some day when she was grown-up she planned to do exactly that same thing. People really seemed to like it a lot.

She checked her script one more time and then looked around for her dad. He wasn't there yet. Amanda sighed. She knew his work often kept him from getting to places on time, especially for fun things like this.

"It's almost time to begin," Beth said softly as she and the other teachers herded all the children to the curtained area they had dubbed as backstage. "Is everyone ready?" she asked.

Every head nodded but no one spoke.

"All right, then. Circle of friendship," Beth prompted.

Amanda and all the other children clasped each other's hands as they formed a circle. They all closed their eyes for a moment until they heard the third-grade teacher's voice say, "Blessings on us all."

"Deep breath," Beth prompted as she demonstrated taking in air and slowly releasing it. "And it's show time," she added with that wonderful smile of hers that made them all feel as if nothing could possibly go wrong.

Amanda stepped out from behind the curtain and into the spotlight. Of course, the spotlight was really just a lamp with a bright bulb in it, but she might as well have been on the biggest stage in the world. Then she saw her father slip into a single empty seat in the front row. He made the motion she often made to him when he sang in the church choir—the one that reminded him to smile. She felt her mouth curve and at the same time she relaxed. Her dad could be such a geek sometimes.

The entire performance seemed to fly by and before she knew it, every class had performed their part and all of the school's thirty-two students and their teachers were standing onstage and bowing to the audience. Meanwhile everyone in the audience was standing and applauding and a few of the rangers were whistling and cheering. It was really something.

"You were just wonderful, Amanda," Dad said as he came onto the stage and hugged her. "Mom would have been so proud of you."

Mom was proud, Amanda thought with pleasure. It was hard to explain to her dad that she often felt that her mom was with her—watching over her, laughing with her, fuming over this or that. Dad didn't much like to talk about things like that—not since Mom died. Amanda really wished she could find some way to make him see that Mom was okay and that just like Reverend Dixon had told them, she was in a better place because in heaven she wasn't sick or in pain anymore.

"I'll get you some punch," Dad told her and moved away just as Beth approached.

Amanda did not miss the fact that he had hurried away just at the time Beth came closer. He did that a lot, but Amanda was sure that he really liked her teacher. It was something grown-ups could be so stupid about. They liked each other but they acted like there was something wrong about that. All of which led her to the conclusion that Beth was special. She smiled at that idea. If Dad thought of Beth as special, then just maybe...

Once she had even hinted to Sara that her dad and Beth might get married. Sara had acted like it was the most amazing idea she'd ever heard.

Amanda went in search of her father. Maybe there was some way she could make sure that he and Beth got a little closer. "Miss Baxter could use a glass of punch," Amanda said as he handed her a cup filled with the rosy-colored liquid. "She's hardly had time to breathe," Amanda added in her best imitation of the way Connie Spinner talked sometimes.

She watched her father watch Beth and saw how his eyes got all soft and mushy when he looked at her. It was the way men looked at ladies on television when you were supposed to understand that they really really liked each other and would probably end up kissing before the next commercial.

"I'll pour her a glass for you to take her," her dad replied.

Amanda had seen that on television too where somebody brings the beautiful lady a drink and then tells her it's from some man sitting clear across the room. She waited until her dad had the full glass in his hand and then she said, "Could you do it, Dad? I just saw Sara and there's something I really need to tell her."

Sara was on the other side of the room but Amanda sprinted toward her, grabbed her and said, "Just pretend that I'm telling you something really serious," she ordered.

Sara's face twisted into a frown of serious concern. Sara was a born actress. Everybody said so. "What's up?" she asked.

"I want Dad to take that punch to Miss Baxter."

The two girls watched as Amanda's father stood holding the punch and looking at Beth. Beth was totally unaware that he was watching her because she was so busy taking care of one of the little kids. But then she looked up, and the first person she looked at was Amanda's dad. The two girls held their breath.

"This is *so* romantic," Sara whispered.

"I know," Amanda agreed. *Take her the punch, Dad.*

Beth smiled and Amanda's dad lifted the punch glass in a kind of a toast like he did on Thanksgiving and New Year's, but he didn't cross the room. He stayed where he was and drank the punch himself.

"I have a surprise for you," Amanda said later that week as she helped Beth clean up after school.

"Really?" Beth was glad that in spite of the fact that Greg had obviously resolved to keep his distance, he hadn't kept Amanda from spending time with her. "I love surprises."

Amanda sighed. "Me, too."

"Well?"

"Tomorrow. I get to go with Dad for his rounds in the park, and he said it would be okay if you came, too."

Beth studied the child. She appeared to be holding her breath. "You asked him if it was all right to bring me?"

Amanda nodded vigorously. "Will you come?"

"I don't know, Amanda...."

"Oh, please say you will. You've been talking about wanting to see the park in winter and now this is only the most perfect chance and Dad said you could come and it could be months before he's not too busy to let us come with him and—"

Beth laughed. "All right, you've talked me into it. I'll call your father tonight to get the time and everything."

"Six o'clock," Amanda assured her. "Dad likes to get going early and then we have the fabulous breakfast on the trail and then we go everywhere—you've just got to see the geysers in winter and then we'll stop for lunch at the winter patrol cabin. Dad will make a fire, and we'll have marshmallows. It's going to be the best day of your whole life, I bet."

"Six?" Beth said. "In the morning? Isn't it still dark then?"

"Yeah. It's so cold you can see your breath and Dad says your words could freeze except for mine. He says I talk way too fast and too much for my words to ever freeze. He brings a big thermos full of hot cocoa, and we sip it along the way. It's just heaven." She sighed as if she had just laid out a trip to a tropical island. "You're just going to love it."

Beth smiled what she hoped was an encouraging smile. She really wanted to see the park in winter. She also wanted to spend time with Greg and get them past this silly impasse. And she very much wanted to make Amanda's day. But, the thought of getting out from under her pile of quilts and dressing in the dark to actually venture outside for most of the day was intimidating, to say the least.

Amanda must have seen her hesitation. "You know, Dad thinks you're a real tenderfoot," she said as she focused all of her attention on cleaning off the chalkboard. "I bet he thinks you'll say no."

Beth knew what Amanda was up to in throwing out this challenge and at the same time her mind conjured up the skeptical face of Greg Stone. The child was right. Greg thought she would make some excuse and refuse to come. That's why he had agreed that Amanda could invite her. He was betting that she would make an excuse and he would win in two ways—he wouldn't have to face her and he wouldn't *lose* face with his daughter.

"Okay, six it is," she said with an enthusiasm she didn't quite feel.

Greg packed supplies into the saddlebags and saddled his horse, then turned his attention to the smaller second horse. Amanda had assured him that her guest could ride although she had remained closemouthed about which of her friends was coming along. In answer to his question as he tucked her in for the night she had just giggled and said, "You're going to be really surprised."

He chuckled to himself as he checked the cap on the thermos of hot chocolate. Whoever she was bringing, it had been too long since he had spent a day with his daughter and he was looking forward to their trip. Earlier, as he lay in bed waiting for the clock to go off, he'd had the thought that every day that passed took them a little further from the pain of Lu's death. Every day brought them a little closer to feeling normal again, whole again.

He thought about Lu as he saddled the second horse and realized that the usual physical ache he had assumed would be a permanent part of remembering her was absent. He paused and conjured her face and her laughter and her voice urging him to take care. He felt the same sense of pleasure and well-being that he felt whenever he thought of sharing a moment with his best friend who had died when they were both thirteen.

His heart lightened with the realization that he had passed into this new stage of his mourning. The guilt and regret were absent, and so was the familiar rage.

"Hi." A muffled voice croaked the single word from just behind him. "Can I help?"

He turned and faced a very good imitation of a creature from outer space. Only the eyes were familiar. "Beth?"

"Don't you dare laugh at me," she warned. "It is cold, and one thing people who grow up in Chicago know is cold and how to dress for it."

He nodded and strolled around her.

"What are you looking at?" she demanded.

"I'm just wondering if you fall down whether we'll be able to set you upright again? Or with all that padding, will we just have to leave you there until we can let some of the air out of all those layers?"

"You *are* laughing at me," she accused.

He couldn't help it. She looked absolutely ridiculous all done up in a bright-purple down jacket that was a couple of sizes too large for her. Most likely she had borrowed it from Connie. She had obviously used the extra room to put on extra sweaters and probably long underwear. He laughed out loud. "What are you doing out here at this hour dressed like that?"

Her large expressive eyes registered surprise and confusion. "I'm going with you. Oh, I get it. You thought I'd chicken out. Well, I'm tougher than you think, Mr. Chief Ranger." She struck a pose with legs planted apart and hands on her hips. "Besides, Amanda said there would be hot cocoa."

He froze in his tracks.

"Well?" she demanded.

Greg had forgotten the question.

"Is there cocoa or not? Because if not then I'm outta here." She turned and took two steps back toward her unit.

"Dad, stop kidding around," Amanda ordered. "There's cocoa," she assured Beth.

"No wonder the kid was being so cagey about who she'd invited," Greg mumbled.

"You didn't know? But I thought she said it was your idea."

Greg shrugged. "She asked if she could bring a friend. I figured she'd ask—"

"Dougie or Sara," Beth said. "Oh Greg, I'm sorry. I really don't have to...I mean if you'd rather I didn't..."

"Dad, you promised," Amanda stepped between them and gazed up at her father.

Greg looked at Beth. "Do you want to come?"

"Do you want me to come?"

More than anything. "I promised Amanda she could bring a friend. You certainly qualify."

It was not exactly the ringing endorsement Beth had hoped for but she would take what she could get. "In that case, which horse is mine?"

Greg gathered his senses enough to reply. "Well, now ordinarily, I would think Reba here would be for you—smaller more delicate. But with all the weight you've added with those clothes, maybe Skydancer here is the better choice." He patted the neck of his horse. "You don't mind carrying a couple of extra pounds, do you, boy?" he said and then couldn't help laughing again.

He saw that she had caught his joke and was definitely not amused. "That's right, I forgot. You're not exactly a morning person, are you?" he teased as he indicated the smaller horse and prepared to help her mount up.

"My sense of humor appears in direct proportion to the hilarity of the joke," she replied as she tried without much success to get her foot high enough to step into the stirrup and swing onto the horse. The problem was all those layers made what was a fairly routine motion impossible. "I could use a hand," she admitted.

"Give me your foot," he said doing absolutely nothing to disguise his laughter at her predicament as he cupped his hands and boosted her onto the horse. "You do ride, don't you?"

"I ride," she replied through gritted teeth as the horse, Reba, pranced and stamped in the snow and Beth held on trying to get her balance.

"Okay, then. Amanda, come on. You ride behind

me, okay?'' He mounted his own steed and then held out his hand to Amanda to pull her aboard.

Beth fumbled with the reins that had gotten twisted. ''Here, let me help,'' Greg said and urged his horse forward until he was next to hers. Greg took off his gloves and leaned very near as he straightened the reins and checked them. Beth was aware that he did not move back right away and looked up and into his eyes.

''Thanks,'' she murmured.

He studied each of her features as if seeing her for the first time.

''Greg?''

''Yeah,'' he said huskily as if they shared one thought, ''we'd better get started.'' He turned to Amanda. ''Ready?''

''Ready,'' she replied with a salute.

''It can get a little bumpy out there,'' he said as he studied Beth. ''You're sure you can do this?''

''I do ride, Greg,'' she assured him. ''Let's go.''

He gently kneed his horse. ''You heard the lady, Skydancer. Lead on.''

Beth gave a little yelp of surprise and hung on as Reba fell into step and kept pace with Skydancer.

As soon as they were out of town, Greg took one of the old service roads that led them through pine forests in a shortcut to the main road that would lead them into the interior of the park. They passed a small canyon and Greg reined in and pointed. Behind her Beth could look down and see the lights of Mammoth twinkling in the distance as the sleepy little town awoke for a new day.

Greg picked up the pace as they headed on past a group of boulders known as the Hoodoos and onto the open plains surrounding Swan Lake. There he stopped again.

"Listen," he whispered.

Silence and a vast landscape surrounded them.

"Look over there," Greg instructed, his voice still low and reverent as he wrapped his arms around Amanda.

Beth turned and saw the sun rising, streaking the sky with color over Sheepeater Cliffs. An eagle soared across the sky.

"Beautiful, isn't it?" Greg said.

Beth nodded. "I was just thinking about something Reverend Dixon said that first Sunday I was here. It was the most glorious autumn morning, and he said it would be impossible for anyone to look at a morning like that and not believe in God."

Greg didn't make any response and Beth realized that he might have taken her statement the wrong way. "I wasn't…I didn't mean to imply…"

"It's okay. I know what you meant."

"But you don't agree." *Was she determined to ruin the morning?* Beth thought as she willed herself to stay quiet.

Amanda glanced up at her father waiting with Beth for what he would say next.

"Nobody appreciates the majesty of this place more than I do, Beth. That will never change. Coming out here and just standing here looking out at a land-scape untouched by humans has brought me enor-mous peace.''

"That's a start," Beth said softly.

"Well, I love this place," Amanda announced.

"Me, too," Beth replied in an awed tone as she took one more look at the sunrise.

When she looked back, Greg was watching her and there was something indefinable in his gaze. What-ever it was, it gave Beth a rush of pure pleasure.

"Got to get going," Greg said reluctantly.

Once again, Beth followed Greg's lead as the horses cantered across the snow-covered terrain. What was happening to her? She'd been here such a short time, and yet it seemed as if the life she had known before was in the far distant past. This was her reality now, her life now—this place, this man.

By the time they made their next stop, Beth was ravenous, but Greg was focused on his work. He frowned as he caught sight of some indentations in the snow.

"Bear?" she asked nervously.

"Poachers," he said more to himself than to her. He helped Amanda to dismount and then slid off his horse. Beth followed suit. Greg bent and examined the foot impressions and hoofprints. "Recent." He took out his binoculars and scanned the horizon for signs of men on horseback.

Poachers brought to mind tales of the Old West when men had routinely crossed property lines and stolen livestock from their neighbors. "Surely, in this day and age…"

Greg's attention turned to her. "It's a wilderness, Beth. It attracts all kinds—those who respect its population and those who don't."

"But there are laws—hunting permits, boundaries."

Greg gave her a wry smile and she saw that his eyes expressed a deep sadness. "Some people don't think the law applies."

The impression of at least two different pairs of boots was unmistakable. "What will you do?"

Greg scanned the horizon. "They've got several hours on us." He pulled his two-way radio from the pack behind him. "Brent?"

Static punctuated the crystal clear air.

"Yeah, boss."

Greg reported the poachers to Brent Moser and turned his attention back to Beth and Amanda. "Can't a guy get anything to eat around this place?" he demanded in mock anger.

Amanda giggled. "Breakfast," she announced as she reached up and retrieved a canvas pack and the thermos of hot cocoa from the saddlebags.

Out of the bag came the most delicious cinnamon rolls that Beth had ever tasted along with bananas, trail mix and the blessed hot chocolate.

"Heaven," she praised as she bit into a roll. "These are incredible."

Amanda grinned. "They're Dad's specialty. He

used to make them all the time before—'' She paused and glanced at Greg, suddenly unsure of herself.

"Before," Greg continued gently. "When Mom was still living. She really loved them."

Amanda's face brightened. "Yeah. She used to say they were absolutely *sinful,* and she'd get the icing all over her chin just like you have now, Beth." Amanda giggled as Beth hastily reached for a paper napkin.

"Got it," Greg said huskily as he gently stroked her chin and caught the dollop of frosting with his bare finger.

Beth felt herself blush but she could not take her eyes off him even when she was aware that Amanda was staring at them both.

"Mom also said that she would never trust a woman who wouldn't eat one of these rolls," Greg said.

"Yeah," Amanda recalled, "she said that anybody who was more interested in their weight or how they looked than eating such a delectable treat was absolutely not to be trusted." Amanda's voice took on an adult quality that was no doubt a perfect imitation of her mother's inflection.

"What did she say about a woman who asked for seconds?" Beth asked, her eyes still locked on Greg's.

He grinned. "The question never came up. Nobody can eat more than one…so far." He was throwing out a challenge.

"Yeah, nobody can eat two," Amanda chorused catching onto the game.

"Oh, really," Beth replied as she fingered another of the giant rolls. She lifted it and took a small bite. "It's very good," she commented as she took a second bite. "Sinfully delicious," she added as she took a third.

With each bite she took, Greg's eyes widened. "You'll make yourself sick," he warned.

"But I'm not breaking any park rules or anything, am I?" she asked as she took another tiny bite.

"Come on, Beth," Amanda cheered, jumping up and down and clapping her hands.

Beth was having a lot of trouble making a real dent in the roll, which seemed to get bigger rather than smaller with each bite she took.

"Your bites are getting smaller," Greg noted with satisfaction. "We'll be here all day if you eat at that pace. Give it up, Beth, and let's get back on the trail."

Beth forced herself to take a larger bite. She was beginning to understand the perils of gluttony, but she was determined to win the challenge. "Let's make this contest a little more interesting," she said. "If I finish it, what do I get?"

Greg roared with laughter and Beth thought her heart would leap right out of her chest with the thrill of hearing him laugh with such abandon. "An enormous stomachache for starters."

Beth shrugged as she carefully wrapped the remainder of the roll and put it in the pocket of her jacket.

"Ah, don't give up," Amanda protested.

"I'm not," Beth replied. "It occurs to me that there were no rules about time so I assume that as long as I finish eating the roll by, say the time we get back to town, I'll have met the challenge?"

"You can't...that's not the way..." Greg sputtered.

Beth grinned and put her arm around Amanda. "You had your chance to lay out the rules. Too bad, so sad. Now, weren't you anxious for us to get going here?"

Greg muttered something under his breath that Beth was certain was best not heard by herself or Amanda. She winked at Amanda and the two of them toasted each other with cups of hot cocoa.

Once they were back on their horses, Beth realized that Greg was traveling at a much slower rate. She knew that he was still on the lookout for signs of the poachers even though he kept up a lively commentary, indicating points of interest as they traveled through the park. An hour later, he reined Skydancer in hard, knowing Reba would follow his lead and stop as well.

"Stay here," he said tersely as he lifted Amanda onto Beth's horse and guided Skydancer toward a clump of trees.

"Some people just don't understand," Amanda explained as she watched Skydancer break a path through the powdery knee-deep snow. "They aren't bad people, really. They just don't understand."

Beth put her arm around the little girl as they both

watched Greg reach the trees. He knelt, then stood and pulled out his two-way radio again. They couldn't hear the conversation but everything about his body language said that he had found something he didn't like.

As Skydancer followed his own footsteps back to them Greg scanned the sky. The wind had picked up, and the gray day had gotten noticeably darker. "There's a storm on the way," he said. "We'd better head for shelter."

"What's over there, Dad?" Amanda motioned toward the clump of trees.

"The poachers killed a moose for the antlers," he replied.

"Did you call Brent?" Amanda asked as if this were nothing new.

Greg nodded.

Tears glistened on Amanda's cheeks. "I hate those bad men, Dad," she whispered. "I know that's wrong, but I can't help it. They are bad."

Greg glanced up at Beth. He seemed at a loss to know what to say.

Beth hugged Amanda. "It's really hard to understand these things sometimes, Amanda, even for grown-ups." She looked up at Greg and saw that he was as deeply saddened as his daughter was by the senseless killing of the moose.

"We'll get them, honey," Greg promised.

Amanda's lips tightened. "I just don't understand it. We're all God's creatures, isn't that right, Beth?"

"Yes, even the bad guys."

Amanda blinked in disbelief and she opened her mouth to protest that remark.

"Remember what we talked about in school," Beth reminded her quietly.

Greg watched them both with interest. "What?" he asked.

"It's important not to get angry at others when they do something we don't understand," Amanda said.

"I see," Greg replied but clearly he didn't see at all.

"These men made a very bad decision today, Amanda," Beth said. "They may have thought they had a good reason even though we know they didn't."

Amanda nodded. "We'll just have to educate them," she said with a very grown-up sigh of exasperation. "Right, Dad?"

Greg looked from his daughter to Beth and back again. "Right," he agreed even though he was obviously still unconvinced. He studied the darkening sky. "Come on. Let's get the two of you to the patrol cabin."

The horses seemed to fly across the snow as Greg set his sights on the sheltered cabin the rangers used as an outpost for some of their winter duties. They both reined the horses to a halt near the front door.

"You two unload the stuff while I get the place opened up." He unlocked and opened the thick shutters, then headed around the side of the small cabin and returned a few minutes later with his arms loaded with firewood.

The one-room cabin had been recently used as evidenced by the fact that the snow had been shoveled away from the door. Inside everything was in pristine condition, and Beth took notice of how well stocked the cabin was with cans of food, blankets, reading materials and a two-way radio. A ladder in one corner of the room led to a loft space.

"Sometimes a patrol can get snowed in for several days," Greg explained when she commented on the variety of canned goods lining the shelves. "We'll probably be here for the night—or at least the two of you will."

She took notice of the four kitchen matches laid out in order on the edge of the stove.

"The last occupant is responsible for making sure there is kindling and that matches are laid out ready to start a fire," Greg explained. "In the cold and dark, it's imperative that a ranger be able to feel for the match and get the fire going as quickly as possible."

His brow furrowed and she had the urge to brush it smooth with her fingertips. He looked tired and worried. "We'll be fine," she assured him.

"I have work to do, and as long as Amanda can stay with you I won't have to ruin her day. Do you mind? I may not get back tonight," he said.

"It's all right," she assured him and turned to Amanda. "Top bunk or lower one?" she asked.

"Top," Amanda declared with a grin. "Can we make s'mores?"

"Possibly, if a certain young lady eats every bite of her dinner."

"Canned beef stew?" Amanda looked skeptical.

"Not your favorite?" Beth asked.

Amanda made a face and both Greg and Beth laughed.

"To tell you the truth," Beth confided, "it's not exactly at the top of my list, either, but then we pioneer women can't be picky. We must be brave and keep the home fires burning, right?"

"And make s'mores?" Amanda added hopefully.

"And make s'mores," Beth agreed.

Greg smiled. "Let me show you how to keep the fire going."

Beth rolled her eyes. "Another lecture," she muttered and grinned at him.

After Greg had shown Beth the basics, he pulled on his parka and gloves. "You'll be fine," he said as if he needed to assure himself.

But will you? she thought but didn't want to ask questions with Amanda there.

"He'll be okay," Amanda promised her and Beth wondered at the little girl's instincts for reading grown-up minds.

Beth stood at the door of the cabin with her arm around Amanda. The little girl waved to her father as he mounted Skydancer and took off after the poachers.

Beth truly felt like a pioneer homesteader watching her man ride off into the sunset. "Keep him safe," she murmured as he crossed a rise and disappeared from sight.

Chapter Eleven

It took Greg three hours to track the poachers to where they had crossed the park boundary back into Montana. They would be back no doubt, but there was little he or the other rangers could do but patrol the boundary on as regular a basis as possible until the poachers returned.

That was a good plan but the problem was, the park was understaffed. Funding for extra rangers in the winter months had never been a priority even though Greg had gone to Washington himself to present their case to a senate subcommittee. He took one last look around to see if the poachers had left any evidence that might be helpful in identifying them, then mounted Skydancer and headed back toward the patrol cabin.

As he rode along, he considered the thought that had come to him early that morning. He was no longer mourning for Lu. He would always miss her, but the long period of mourning was over. He examined his thoughts and felt only complete comfort. Lu had been gone now for nearly two years. He had coped by focusing everything on his work. Lately that hadn't seemed like enough, and he had compensated by taking on even more work.

Then Beth had arrived. From the first she had made him feel things that made him uncomfortable in her presence. He sensed something about her that spelled danger or risk. He had been determined to keep his distance and had failed miserably.

In spite of his best efforts, in spite of the impossibility of the entire idea, he was struggling mightily against falling in love with her. And yet loving her was not an option—for either of them. There were so many problems, any one of which might have been surmountable, but taken together they spelled trouble.

Even so, he couldn't wait to see her, to get back to the cabin where she would be waiting for him. The very image of that made him smile and push Skydancer even harder. He imagined her with Amanda, the two of them playing some card game or reading a story or perhaps baking something. His visions of domestic bliss made the trip go faster. He chose not to ruin his fantasies by considering what the future might hold. For now, he wanted to savor the moment—the day he had awakened to find the familiar ache in his heart healed and had known that he could love again.

An hour's distance from the cabin it started to

snow—a light steady fall that he knew meant they were in for several inches before dawn. He pressed on.

It'll be good to be home, he thought and it stunned and pleased him to realize that by *home* he meant wherever Beth and Amanda were. His feelings were deepening by the hour, much like the snow around him.

It was dark when he crossed the last ridge. He was relieved to see smoke coming from the chimney, meaning Beth had managed to keep the fire going. He was mystified to see the addition of several small bonfires around the perimeter of the cabin. "Come on, Skydancer, let's get down there and see what this incredible, if sometimes slightly crazy, woman is up to now."

As soon as he reined in Skydancer and dismounted, Beth and Amanda opened the door to the cabin and Amanda rushed out to meet him. Beth's eyes were wide with relief. Amanda's were equally alive with excitement.

"There was a bear, Dad," she announced as she flung herself at him and hugged him hard. "And the wolves were howling and howling and howling. Beth built fires like the pioneers used to when they traveled west on the wagon trains."

Beth had not moved. She was smiling, but it was the sort of tight, brave smile that did not reach her eyes.

Greg pulled Amanda next to him and walked toward the house. "You okay?" he asked Beth.

She nodded but seemed paralyzed with fear.

"Honey, why don't you fix me some tea?" he said to Amanda who rushed to do his bidding. He turned his attention back to Beth. "Come here," he said softly as he pried her fingers away from the door frame and hugged her hard.

She gave a shuddering sob and buried her face against his shoulder. "I thought... I was so afraid that..."

"Sh-h-h. I'm here now. It's okay." He stroked her hair and waited for the shivers that racked her body to subside.

"He was a monster," Amanda said as she brought the tea—a cup for him and one for Beth, as well. "We were pretty scared, but Beth told me stories about women who went west in the old days and how sometimes they had to be the ones who kept the home fires burning, right?"

"That's right," Beth replied with a weak smile as she wrapped her shaking hands around the mug of tea and let the steam bathe her face.

"Where did you see the bear?" Greg asked. Sometimes bears would try to break into the cabin for the rations. He mentally berated himself for not preparing Beth for that possibility.

"We heard the wolves first and then they just kept it up and we couldn't decide if they were coming closer," Amanda explained. "Then we decided to build the campfires while it was still light. Beth did a great job, didn't she, Dad?"

"I thought I'd get back sooner," he said. "I'm

sorry." He sat beside her, rubbing her back, trying to ease the tension that bunched the muscles of her shoulders and neck.

Beth looked up at him, her eyes calm and lovely. "It's okay," she replied and managed another smile that was a little closer to her usual sunny grin. "We frontier women are tough, aren't we, Amanda?"

"How did you come up with the campfire idea?" Greg asked, his own mood lightening in direct proportion to hers.

"I saw it in a movie," she admitted. "It was probably dumb."

"Not at all. It showed real initiative."

"Dad is real big on initiative," Amanda confided as if Greg had suddenly gotten up and left the room. "He'll even forgive a mistake if you at least show some imagination."

"I'll have to remember that." Beth looked at Greg who was grinning at her. "The bear was up on the rise just sort of standing there, watching us." She shivered.

"It gave us the williams, right Beth?"

"Willies," Beth corrected gently. "It gave us the willies."

"Did he come closer?" Greg asked, his expression filled with concern and worry.

"No. Maybe the fires helped?"

Greg shrugged and then he grinned. "Obviously it beats singing and blowing a whistle."

"Dad! That's just mean," Amanda chastised him. Beth laughed and once she started she seemed unable to stop. "Maybe a whistle should be standard equipment here in the cabin," she said between bursts of laughter.

Then Amanda started to giggle and Greg started to laugh and before long the three of them were collapsed onto the bunk that served as bed and sofa for the tiny cabin. Finally, they got control of themselves and the atmosphere in the room returned to normal.

"You must be starving," Beth said as she pushed herself off the bunk and headed toward the small cookstove. "I made the stew," she said proudly.

"And biscuits," Amanda added proudly pointing to a pan of biscuits that were flat and unevenly cooked.

"Smells terrific and I am famished. Let me just take care of Skydancer and wash up."

While they ate, he filled them in on the hunt for the poachers. He tried to downplay the danger for Amanda's sake, but he saw that Beth understood that he had been at perhaps even greater risk than she had that long afternoon. It touched him to see the concern in her eyes and at the same time he wanted to reassure her that he knew how to handle himself in these situations.

"I have a good crew," he said.

"I know." She focused on clearing the dishes.

"We know what we're doing," he added.

She nodded and her hand shook slightly as she scraped a plate. "It's just really the first time I've thought about there being danger from humans," she said softly. "Somehow that's different from the animals."

"Yeah, I know. It's easier to forgive the animals. They're just doing what they have to do to survive."

"Maybe these men are, as well," Beth suggested.

"I doubt that."

"We really don't know. They could be out of work and looking for a way to feed their families or pay their rent," she said.

Greg studied her. "You have this knack for always seeing the good, don't you?"

It wasn't a reprimand, but she understood that her ability to look for the reasons behind acts of destruction or misfortune bewildered him.

Amanda yawned noisily.

"Bedtime, scamp," he said.

"Aw, Dad," she protested but stumbled over to the bunk beds and sat on the lower one to take off her shoes.

Greg helped her get ready for bed and lifted her onto the top bunk. He pulled the rough blanket over her, topped it with a down sleeping bag and kissed her good-night. "Love you," he murmured.

"Me too, love you," she mumbled and was asleep.

Beth watched the scene play out and felt tears sting her eyes. It was so wonderful to see them both safe, to know that Greg was there in case the bear or wolves returned.

"Hey, what's this?" he said softly as he turned away from his sleeping daughter and saw her tears.

"I really don't know," she replied with a shaky laugh. "Just a long day, I guess."

"I really appreciate the way you watched after Amanda today, Beth."

"She did as much for me."

"I know you must have been so frightened, and I'm sorry. I should have prepared you for some of the possibilities."

"You had your work to think about. In the end we were fine."

"But you were scared."

She nodded and the tears came in earnest. "And I was worried about you," she admitted. She knew it was the release of all the tension and anxiety she had endured through the long afternoon and evening, but her inability to stop blubbering was embarrassing nevertheless. "This is stupid," she said and brushed impatiently at the tears.

"Come here," he said and for the second time that night she walked straight into his embrace.

They stood in the middle of the small rustic cabin, their arms around each other as he rocked her slowly from side to side. Undone by this gentler side of him focused entirely on her, she continued to cry. Her tears soaked the front of his flannel shirt.

"Hey," he coaxed and gently lifted her chin with his forefinger so that she was looking up at him. "It's all right," he assured her and she saw that he wanted to kiss her.

"Greg," she whispered and stroked his cheek.

He bent to meet her lips and they shared their first

kiss—a kiss of such gentle tenderness that they were each struck by its fragility and preciousness. Beth could feel his heart pounding beneath her palm and knew that her own heart beat in unison with his. She was a woman who had led a charmed life. Yet, never before had she felt so cherished.

When the kiss ended, he continued to hold her, his lips resting against her temple, his breath a gentle breeze on her hair.

There is something so right about all of this, Greg Stone. I don't know where we will end up, but we are connected. God has brought us together at a time when we each needed a friend. Whatever happens next, I'm putting my trust in Him and so should you, she thought, but knew if she said the words aloud, it would startle Greg and spoil this moment—a moment she knew she would treasure for the rest of her life.

"You must be exhausted," he said finally and stepped back but continued to rest his hands loosely on her shoulders.

"I am a little wiped out," she admitted. She glanced at Amanda sleeping peacefully in the upper bunk and then at the lower bunk. She could not control the blush that stained her cheeks as she realized that there were two of them and only one remaining bed.

"There's a sleeping bag," he said as if reading her mind. Then he cleared his throat as she had learned was his habit whenever he was uncomfortable with the way things were going. "I should bring in some wood for the fire."

"I'll help. After all, I was the one who used up the supply setting those ridiculous fires." She reached for her parka.

"Stay here. Maybe heat up the last of the cocoa. I'll get the wood." His voice had taken on that tense tone he sometimes used with her.

"I'll—"

He opened the door and she was silenced by the sudden influx of bitter cold and snow. The wind howled—or was that the wolves?

"Be careful," she said as the door blew shut behind him.

In seconds she heard the steady beat of the ax splitting logs. She stood at the cabin's front window and watched him work. He attacked the logs with a fierceness that was both thrilling and a little intimidating. She wondered what he was thinking, and thought she probably knew. Kissing her had been a mistake—a betrayal of his beloved wife.

Beth turned away from the window and checked on the sleeping child. Then she poured the remainder of the cocoa into a small pan and heated it on the stove. She couldn't imagine how they were going to get through this night. They had made real progress toward forging a friendship, but the kiss had changed everything. Where would they go from here?

She heard the steady rhythmic beat of Greg splitting the logs and then silence, followed by the sound of him stamping snow off his boots at the door to the cabin. She hurried to open the door for him.

"I made the cocoa," she said for lack of anything else to say.

He nodded and stacked the firewood near the stove. Then he pulled a length of rope from his parka pocket and tied one end to the post of the bunk beds just below where Amanda slept.

"What's that?" Beth asked as she divided the cocoa between two mugs and handed one to him.

"Privacy." He fixed the other end of the rope to the other bedpost. Then he draped a blanket across it curtain-style. "You're not the only one who learns from going to the movies," he explained.

Beth smiled. "Clark Gable and Claudette Colbert."

"Normally I would sleep up there in the loft, but given what you've been through, I'll camp out on the sleeping bag over there on the floor, and you—"

He grimaced as he tightened the rope.

"What's wrong?"

To her surprise, he smiled—it was a sheepish grin, but a smile nonetheless and it seemed as if the tension that had crowded into the small space with them since they kissed had eased.

"It's been a while since I chopped wood," he admitted. "I've rubbed a doozy of a blister."

Beth held his hand and examined his palm. "My heavens, Greg. What were you thinking?"

He covered her hand with his, forcing her to look up at him. "I was thinking about you…us. What were you thinking while I was out there playing macho man?"

Beth ducked her head shyly. "Same thing," she admitted. "I'm sorry…" She began.

"We need to talk," he said at the same time.

"You first."

He looked at her. "What have you got to be sorry about?"

"I…falling apart…being so silly…"

"That's not why I kissed you."

"It started out that way."

"Yes," he agreed, "but it changed."

"How?"

Her eyes searched his expression for clues to his mood.

"I wanted to," he said softly and caressed her face with his injured hand.

She closed her eyes and savored his touch.

"I want to again," he added softly.

She nodded. "But we shouldn't," she said finishing what she was certain he was thinking. "Not until we figure a few things out."

"Such as?"

"You're the one who has set limits," she reminded him.

He sighed heavily. "We can't ignore the fact that you are only here for a few months, Beth."

"You see, that's one of the differences between us," she replied. "You focus on my leaving and I think about the time I am here—now, tomorrow, next month."

He nodded. "But if we let our feelings…if we give in to…we have to consider Amanda."

"I am considering Amanda. She's happy. She likes me. She likes doing things with me and with you. What's wrong with that?"

"Nothing at all, as long as that's as far as it goes."

"And what if it went further?"

"We both understand that there's another piece of this that has nothing to do with Amanda," he said.

Beth nodded. "Faith," she said. "Belief." She felt him tense.

Their fingers intertwined and neither of them seemed to know what to say.

"Where do you keep the first-aid kit?" she asked huskily.

"On the shelf next to the door," he replied but did not release his hold on her.

"What if we tried it again—kissing?"

Beth looked up at him in surprise. She smiled. She knew he was only trying to lighten the mood. He was a man, after all, and there had been that spark of something between them. He was flirting with her.

She lifted his wounded hand to her lips. She could feel his eyes on her as she tenderly kissed his palm. "You mean like this?"

"That's a start."

"And that's as far as we're going to go," she said lightly. "I'll get the first-aid kit." The one thing she knew she couldn't handle was any kind of casual affair between them.

This time he let her go.

As expected the kit was well-stocked and in no time she had cleaned the wound and applied a soothing ointment. She wrapped his hand loosely in gauze. As she worked he sipped his cocoa and said nothing.

"There. That should help." She replaced all the materials in the first-aid kit and returned it to the shelf. *Now what?* She thought nervously.

"I'm going out to check the horses," he said shrugging into his parka. "Why don't you go ahead and get ready for bed?"

She understood that he was actually leaving to give her some privacy for performing her bedtime routine. The cabin had a portable toilet, and Amanda had shown her how to melt snow and heat it for washing herself. There was a kettle filled with steaming water on the back of the stove.

By the time Greg returned she was just getting under the covers of the lower bunk.

"All set?" he asked as he sat on the edge of the bed and tucked her in.

She nodded.

"Good night then," he said huskily and bent to kiss her forehead. "Thank you again for taking care of Amanda, Beth. I honestly don't know what I would have done without you."

"We make a good team," was all she could think to say. "I mean, Amanda and me."

He smiled and brushed a strand of hair away from her cheek. "I know what you mean, Beth. I think we make a good team, as well—the three of us. Amanda and I are both lucky to have you as our friend. Good night."

Beth knew that she should be thrilled at his compliment. He was telling her that they were friends. Friendships could last across the miles. Friends visited each other from time to time. For the first time since she had met him, he wasn't reminding her that she was leaving in a few months. Still, the confession that they were friends led to the obvious understanding that that was all they were—or ever could be.

He stood and pulled the blanket curtain into place. She heard him stoke the fire and spread the sleeping bag. She heard him take off his heavy boots and settle in for the night.

Remembering the kiss, she put her fingers to her lips and wondered how they were going to manage the next several months.

Chapter Twelve

Beth woke to the sound of voices and horses snorting and stamping outside the cabin. She also recognized the smell of bacon frying and biscuits baking. Light seemed to flood the cabin through the small window. In the bunk above her, Amanda grumbled and pulled the covers over her head.

Beth peeked out from the cocoon created by the blanket curtain and blinked rapidly as she tried to adjust to the sudden glare of the light.

"Rise and shine," Greg called out. "We've got company."

Beth noticed that he was fully dressed, the sleeping bag had been cleared away and he was stirring something on the stove. He had removed the gauze that covered his blistered palm.

"Dad, it's not a school day. I get to sleep in," Amanda protested in a muffled voice from under the covers.

Greg slid the pot to one side and headed for the door. "Two women in my life who aren't morning persons may be more than I can handle," he commented and laughed when both Beth and Amanda protested the sudden influx of cold air that accompanied his opening the door. "Come on in, guys. Coffee's on," he called cheerfully.

Beth suddenly realized that there were people outside who would soon be inside and she was still in bed. She scrambled to her feet and tried to straighten the tangled knot of the clothes she'd slept in. It was hopeless. Her sweatpants were twisted around her legs and the socks were half on with the toes flopping crazily with each step she took.

"Morning, Beth."

Brent ducked his head to clear the doorway as he entered the cabin. He was followed closely by Todd Roberts, another ranger. "Sorry to disturb you."

Beth realized how this must look to the two rangers. She wondered how she could possibly explain that it had all been platonic. She looked to Greg for help and realized he would be no help at all. The man knew exactly what she was thinking, and he was enjoying her discomfort.

"Let me get you some coffee," she said as the two rangers took off their parkas and gloves.

She handed them each a mug of coffee and poured one for herself.

"The poachers came back last night," Brent told Greg and in that one sentence he erased all trace of Greg's good mood.

"I was afraid of that when I heard you coming. Did they make a hit?"

Todd nodded. "Yes, sir. A bull elk."

Not my bull elk, Beth wanted to protest. Her hand shook as she served up the eggs, biscuits and bacon.

"The trail is still really fresh. They must have come in early this morning," Brent continued. "The snow will slow them down quite a bit."

"You think we can get them?" Greg studied the younger rangers. "There's no time to get backup in place before we go."

"Yes, sir, I do. We'll have to act fast but I'm sure we can," Brent replied.

"Let's get going then," Greg said as he tossed back the last of his coffee and reached for his parka. "Amanda?"

A tousled head popped out from beneath the covers. Clearly, Amanda had been listening. "Yes, Dad."

"Time to go."

Instantly, Amanda was off the bunk, dressing and packing her gear. Beth helped her finish dressing and insisted she eat some breakfast. "Five minutes," she told Greg.

He turned back to confer with the two rangers. They spoke in low urgent tones and Beth realized that with the poachers still out there, even five minutes was asking a lot.

"You two go on. I'll take Beth and Amanda back to town and come in from the other direction," Greg instructed. He held up his two-way radio. "Stay in touch," he added as the rangers bundled up and left the cabin.

"Hurry, Amanda. We need to get started," Beth said softly as she checked to be sure that the matches were in place for the cabin's next visitors.

Amanda shoved the rest of a biscuit in her mouth and grabbed her parka. Beth had just washed the last of the morning dishes and replaced them on the shelf when Greg returned from closing and locking the shutters.

He glanced around the cabin checking for the matches and kindling and saw that everything was in order. "Good work," he said and pulled Amanda's hood into place and fastened it under her chin. "Are you ready to ride, partner?" he asked with a grin.

"Yep," Amanda replied and headed for the door.

Beth saw that in spite of the smile he had given his daughter, Greg's expression was grim. He was frustrated that the poachers had struck again. "I wish there was something I could do," she offered.

He wrapped his arm around her shoulder as they headed outside together. "There is. Once we reach town, could you take care of Amanda until I get back? It could be a couple of days."

"Of course." She would have walked over hot coals for the man. Asking her to care for Amanda was like giving her a gift instead of asking a favor.

Greg checked one last time to be sure that the cabin was secure. He had saddled the horses, and they stood ready and waiting as if they, too, understood the urgency. Beth mounted her horse and waited while Greg lifted Amanda onto his and got on behind her.

"All set?"

Beth gave him the thumbs-up sign and he nodded and headed out. Reba trotted to keep up with Sky-dancer's pace.

Beth understood that this would be no leisurely trip to catch a glimpse of the park's winter garb. Instead, everything flew by as if the world had suddenly been thrown into fast-forward as they moved from trot to full gallop. Amanda closed her eyes and hung on.

They had been riding for some time when Beth realized Greg was slowing down. She looked up and saw a rider coming toward them.

"It's Brent," Greg shouted.

"We've spotted them," Brent reported as soon as the two horses were parallel. Both men dismounted and walked a little away. Beth followed suit telling Amanda to stay with the horses.

"Todd's keeping watch but they're pretty close to the border—playing it cagey," Brent reported.

"Did they spot you?"

Brent shook his head. "I think we stand a good chance of surrounding them and getting them with the evidence before they can get out of the park." Once caught, the rangers would take the poachers back to Mammoth where they would be kept in jail until they could appear before the U.S. magistrate who served the park.

Greg nodded and turned his attention to Beth. "Do

you think you can take Amanda on Reba there and make it back to town?''

Beth glanced nervously at the vast white wilderness surrounding them and nodded.

As usual he had read her mind and he took a step closer. ''We'll get you to a marked trail. I'll radio ahead and have one of the rangers start out from town and meet you. As long as you follow the markers, you'll be fine.''

Beth nodded again.

''You do know I wish there were some other way,'' he said.

''I know. We'll be fine. Don't worry about Amanda. I'll take good care of her.''

''For once I should be seeing that someone takes care of you,'' he said and touched her cheek.

''It's okay,'' she managed to say around the lump of emotion that had formed in her throat. He helped Amanda onto Reba, and Beth pasted on her bravest smile. It would not do to panic now. Greg had promised a marked trail, and she believed him. It didn't matter that everywhere she turned everything looked the same. She would follow the markers and before she knew it they would be home.

''Ready for a new adventure?'' she asked Amanda with a heartiness she really did not feel.

''Cool,'' Amanda shouted once Greg had explained the plan.

''Don't rush,'' Greg advised as they stood next to the horses. ''You've got plenty of daylight.'' He pulled out his radio and called headquarters. She heard the instructions to send someone on the trail. Then he pulled Beth a little away from Brent and Amanda. "I'm going to make this up to you. I know that I've got to stop counting on you to be there for Amanda and me."

"Because I'll be leaving," she finished his thought.

"Because it's not fair," he corrected. "If there was any other choice..."

"We'll be fine. Really." She wanted to reassure him. She wanted to touch his haggard face. She wished there were more she could do to make it easier for him to do the job he needed to do.

"I'll make it up to you," he promised again.

She laughed. "I'll hold you to that. For somebody who thought I was a rank tenderfoot a few weeks ago, you sure are putting me to the test," she teased.

Her reward was his smile. "I may have jumped to some incorrect assumptions," he admitted sheepishly. "On the other hand, you were singing to a bear and later on I caught you arguing with an elk. You have to admit that's pretty questionable behavior." He reached to embrace her then, aware of the others, changed his mind and withdrew his hand. "I have to go."

"I know. Don't worry. Amanda will be fine. I won't let anything happen to her." She didn't want him thinking about them when he needed to focus all his attention on what was potentially a dangerous situation. "Just take care of you," she added.

This time he did stroke her cheek with his gloved finger.

Beth reached up and covered his hand with her own. "You'd better get going. Brent keeps glancing at the horizon as if he's expecting the enemy to come over that rise at any moment."

Greg laughed as they walked back toward the others. Brent was already on his horse and had helped Amanda transfer from Skydancer to Reba. Greg helped Beth onto Reba more because he needed to touch her than because she needed the help. Then he mounted Skydancer and signaled for her to follow them.

"Here goes nothing," she muttered to herself as she urged Reba onto the trail Skydancer was breaking. Amanda was smiling as if she were on some grand adventure.

Too soon they reached the trailhead. Without breaking Skydancer's pace, Greg motioned toward the marker, and Beth signaled that she saw it and understood. Greg waved and took off, but Beth noticed that he watched over his shoulder to be sure that they were safely started on the trail.

As she navigated the trail, she replayed the sight of him riding off like some warrior into battle. Once again, she was afraid for him. What if the poachers had guns? What if they had spotted Todd and taken him hostage? What if something happened to Greg?

Watch over him and bring him home safe, she prayed silently. She glanced at Amanda and felt a renewed determination. Her job was to make sure she got the spunky little girl home. There, they would wait together for Greg's return.

* * *

Greg was glad that conversation was not an option as he and Brent rode hard toward the point where he expected the poachers to be. He needed to focus on what lay ahead, but thoughts of Beth kept crowding in around his concentration on the job to be done. Beth standing in the doorway of the cabin. Beth facing her fears so that Amanda would not be harmed. Beth overcome by tears of stress and tension. Beth in his arms. Beth's lips meeting his. Beth tenderly dressing his blister. Beth sleeping. Beth waking. Beth. Beth.

What if there was some possibility they could have a future? What if she stayed after the year was up? Why would she do that? What could he offer her?

Brent Moser signaled him as he turned off the main trail. Greg almost missed the cut. He shook his head, willing himself to pay attention to his duty. The poachers would be armed. They would not surrender willingly. They had too much to lose.

Minutes later, Brent slowed his horse to a walk. Absolute quiet surrounded them. It was impressive and at the same time, eerie. In a place where peace and quiet were commonplace, this quiet seemed too perfect, almost artificial. Brent spoke in low tones on the two-way radio.

"Todd has our position, sir," he reported. "The poachers are working along the north boundary as we suspected."

"How many are there?"

"Only two."

Greg nodded. "Radio for extra backup to help with the arrest and transport and let's go in."

Brent did as he was told. "Todd reports that he called for the extra rangers, and they should be in position."

Greg held out his hand for the radio. "Good work, Todd."

"Thank you, sir." The ranger's voice crackled through the static. "We're ready at this end."

"Then let's go. Give us twenty minutes to get into position on this side and then make your move." He handed the radio back to Brent and motioned for the younger ranger to follow him.

The fact was, Greg loved his work. He couldn't imagine living and working anywhere other than the parks—maybe not Yellowstone forever, but the wilderness was his calling. If anything were to develop between them, how would Beth adjust to that?

A sense of alarm that escalated with every minute gnawed at Beth as she strained to see through the lightly falling snow. She tried to recall the topographical map Greg had brought her. This trail had been the one he showed her. She tried to recall the landmarks he had noted. Had she passed the place where the trail split off to the falls? Had she come to the small cluster of mud pots yet?

The last trail marker had been slightly askew, and she had made a choice and turned to the right. Maybe she should have gone straight. Maybe not. Surely there should be a marker soon. She squinted, trying to see any sign of color in the relentless white-gray-and-brown landscape.

She glanced at the sky, which had grown steadily darker in the last half hour. She slowed Reba to a walk and considered her options.

"Are we lost?" Amanda asked.

Beth looked at the child. She was perfectly calm. The question had been delivered in a matter-of-fact tone that signaled her certainty of the answer.

"Maybe," Beth hedged.

"So, what's the plan?" Amanda looked at Beth with such complete confidence that Beth swallowed her fear and smiled.

"Well, there are a number of possibilities."

"We could go back to the marker," Amanda suggested.

"That's an idea," Beth agreed but the blowing snow was already covering their tracks. Trying to find their way back might only result in their becoming more lost.

"We could stay here and wait for the ranger to find us."

"That's probably not the best choice," Beth said. She glanced at the sky.

"Yeah, probably not. It's getting late and that means the temperature will drop and with the snow and all we should probably keep moving," Amanda reasoned.

Out of the mouths of babes, Beth thought. In the face of Amanda's absolute certainty that Beth would find a way to get them home came the courage Beth needed to take action. Greg was counting on her.

"Maybe if we make our way to that ridge ahead we can see over a greater distance and figure out where we are. What do you think?"

"Works for me," Amanda agreed. "Maybe we'll see Dad and we can set a flare or send smoke signals. He'll be so-o-o surprised." She giggled with delight.

Beth would have liked to share in her pleasure, but the fact was she was becoming more certain by the moment that such antics might actually be essential to their survival.

Please, God, she prayed, genuinely scared now.

She hoped that the ridge wasn't as far in the distance as it appeared. "Hang on, honey," she called to Amanda as she urged Reba off the trail.

As she rode, her mind raced. At least on the ridge, there were trees. That meant wood for a fire. She could start a fire to keep them warm and perhaps it would also serve as a signal for those who would be looking for them. Trees also meant shelter. Hopefully there would be some good tall evergreens. She could settle Amanda in the shelter of the trees and...

Reba stumbled.

"Is Reba okay?" Amanda asked and this time she didn't sound quite so confident.

Beth nodded. "Maybe we should let her wait here though. The slope might be slippery. Let's gather the extra blankets and some of these supplies, okay?" She fought the sense of rising panic and tried not to think about Greg and how she had failed him in the only task that mattered. Amanda was in danger—from the cold and the elements and it was all Beth's fault.

Amanda looked out toward the ridge and back again. "The snow is getting deeper."

"I know, honey, that's why we need to get going. Here, wrap this around you." Beth handed Amanda a blanket and began stuffing supplies from the saddlebags into a backpack. "Okay, let's go. Just keep walking toward those trees there. I'll be right beside you."

Amanda struck out, but slogging through the freshly fallen snow was exhausting and it took a long time to make any progress at all.

"Beth?" Amanda's voice sounded small and scared in the silence of the wilderness.

"What is it, honey?"

Amanda turned to face Beth and made no attempt to hide the huge tears that trickled down each cheek. "I'm scared," she whispered.

Beth wrapped her arm around Amanda's shoulder. "I know you are, but we're going to be all right. Here, follow in my footsteps. That'll be easier."

"How do you know that we'll be okay?"

"I just know it. God will—"

"I know God is supposed to take care of us, but sometimes I wonder."

"What do you wonder?"

Amanda took a deep breath. "Sometimes I wonder why God lets scary stuff like this happen in the first place—I mean if He's in charge of the whole world and all, then how come—"

Beth stopped and turned Amanda so that they were face-to-face. "Now, listen to me. I believe that there is a reason for everything that happens to us—good things and bad. Sometimes it's very hard to understand that reason but in time we begin to see why it was a part of God's plan for us."

Amanda frowned. "You mean like Mom dying?"

Her words were not delivered with malice or anger and yet they felt like a blow to Beth's psyche. "That, too," she replied through clenched teeth. "Right now though, we need to figure out the best way to get through what's happening to us at this moment, today, and one day we'll be telling our friends and our children and grandchildren about this day and we'll realize that there was a reason for it. But first we have to live it, understand?"

Amanda's teeth had started to chatter. "I guess," she replied but she sounded anything but convinced.

"Okay then, on to the ridge," Beth shouted with a bravado she was far from feeling herself. She stepped off in an exaggerated marching step. "Coming?" she called.

"Coming," Amanda replied and Beth's heart twisted as she looked behind her and saw the little girl bravely following in her footsteps.

Chapter Thirteen

"Call for you, Chief," Brent Moser handed him a two-way radio. "It's Taggert back at dispatch."

Doris Taggert was a park veteran. She had worked with Greg's father and Greg knew if she was asking for him, instead of simply relaying a message through Brent, something important had happened.

"I'm here, Dorie. What's up?"

"Just had a message from Becker. He's traveled almost to the trailhead, and there's no sign of Beth and Amanda."

Greg's heart paused and then started to pound in triple time. "Where's Becker now?"

"Waiting for orders. He thought he might have missed them somehow and radioed to see if they had made it back to town." There was a pause. "They haven't."

"Tell Becker to retrace the trail. I'll come in from the other direction."

"Got it."

Greg and the other rangers carried off the arrest of the poachers without incident and recovered enough hides and antlers to put them in jail for a very long time. Now he sent the others to complete the routine of the arrest while he went in search of Beth and Amanda. As he pushed Skydancer hard, taking short-cuts wherever possible to cut the time and distance, Greg considered the possibilities.

It's probably something simple, he thought, but knew that this was unlikely. He visualized the trail, thinking through every turn of it, counting off the markers in his mind. *Where did you turn off the trail, Beth?* He reached the place where he had left her. The fresh snow had covered the tracks. Greg swore and fought against the renewal of the old familiar bile that God would permit such things to happen to people like Amanda and Beth while He was off letting poachers kill innocent beasts on a whim.

"Why?" he shouted. "Why them? Why do this again?" He knew that what he really meant was *Why do this to me again?*

He felt shame that his thoughts focused on his own pain when Beth and Amanda were out there somewhere.

"Help me," he whispered. "*Come on. We'll work the rest out later. Just help me now. I'm begging You, for their sake.*"

He closed his eyes and sat back on Skydancer. He waited. For what, he didn't know. Perhaps for his racing heart to beat more normally, for his shattered brain to function reasonably again.

And suddenly, he knew exactly where she had made the wrong turn. He saw it in his mind's eye as clearly as if it were spotlighted before him. He had seen the marker at that point earlier in the fall and had made a mental note to have it turned so that it clearly pointed the right way for the cross-country skiers who would rely on it to move them safely through the park in winter. But the snows had come sooner than expected, and he had been distracted by other concerns. The sign had remained untouched... and pointing in the wrong direction.

"Thank you," he whispered raggedly and swiped at the tears that etched the exhausted plains of his face. *"I owe you one."*

He reached the crossroads of the trail, saw the twisted sign and turned Skydancer sharply in the direction he was sure she had followed. As he rode, he found himself continuing his silent entreaties to God to get him to Beth and Amanda before anything happened to them. Unlike when Lu was dying, this time his anger was directed at himself rather than God. This time, if anything happened to them, it would be his fault. His prayers came from deep within his soul.

God, I know I've been away, but Beth's faith in you has always been constant. Don't make her pay for my mistakes, for my lack of faith, for my anger. Please, help me find them before it's too late.

Thunder rumbled in the distance. Greg fought against the urge to curse the heavens. Was this God's response? The sky grew darker in the direction he was headed. He thought of Beth and Amanda and their fear of thunderstorms. It was one thing to face a storm from safe inside a warm solid house. It was quite something else to be lost, cold and probably terrified and have to deal with thunder and lightning as well.

Please, Greg chanted again and again as the wet sleet and snow pelted him, making visibility nearly impossible and travel treacherous. He resisted the urge to bargain with a power greater than himself. In the face of his own inability to find Beth and Amanda, he had resorted to his faith. God had answered that first prayer to help him find the right path. Perhaps He would answer this one as well.

In that moment Greg understood that he had never truly stopped believing. He had only turned his back. If he turned around now, would God still be there for him?

In the unending whiteness of the snow, in the distance, he thought he saw a flash of movement. He reined Skydancer in and impatiently wiped sleet and ice from his face. Was it his imagination?

No. It was a horse. It was Reba. His heart leapt with joy then plummeted again. There was no other sign of life as the first bolt of lightning split the sky.

"I'm so scared, Beth," Amanda shouted shakily above the sound of the wind and thunder.

"I know you are, Amanda. Please be brave for just a little bit longer—just until we reach those trees up there, okay?"

Amanda nodded and her grim little face broke Beth's heart. *Please, let there be another patrol shelter or the town or something we can get to and be safe and warm,* she prayed silently as she willed herself to put one foot in front of the other, breaking a trail for Amanda to follow.

Slowly she made her way up the steep hill working her way in a serpentine pattern to find the easiest route and stretching her hand out to bring Amanda along as she climbed. She heard the rumble of thunder and the howl of the wind in the leafless trees.

As the wind gathered force, the trees began to sway, knocking against each other. They sounded like hollowed bamboo poles tapping out an ominous rhythm.

"Amanda, come here," Beth shouted above the thunder and wind as the first lanky tree lost its fragile grip and fell with a clatter on the hill behind them.

Amanda screamed and raced forward. Beth grabbed her hand and stumbled on a horizontal path hoping to get out of the stand of trees. It was useless. They were completely surrounded. Beth wrapped her arms around the terrified child and dropped them both to the ground as trees fell like dominoes all around them. Even though the weight of the trees was lessened due to their thin diameter and hollowed core, Beth knew that with so many trees falling, she and Amanda were in real danger. Lightning streaked the sky and thunder roared nearby.

Please God, not Amanda, Beth prayed fervently. *What would Greg do if he lost Amanda, too?*

She pulled the child more firmly against her, shielding her with her own body as the storm raged. A tree fell just above their heads followed by another that caught Beth squarely across the shoulders. She bit her lip to keep from crying out as pain rifled down her left arm.

As suddenly as the storm came, it passed, leaving behind a path of felled trees, one terrified little girl and a woman who suddenly found she could not move her left shoulder.

"Are you okay, Amanda?"

"I think so," came the quavering reply. "I'm really cold though and hungry, too."

Beth considered her next move—that was assuming she could move. With her good right hand she checked herself for any other injuries and discovered a small lump in the pocket of her parka. She smiled.

"You know what I just remembered?" Beth asked as she rolled slowly away from Amanda and tried not to let her see how much pain that caused her. "Check my pocket," she encouraged. "Go on."

Amanda got to her knees and reached inside the pocket of Beth's parka. "Dad's cinnamon roll," she cried with delight as she held up the smashed, partially eaten roll as if it were pure gold.

Beth grinned. "Go on. Eat it."

"We'll share."

"No, you go ahead. I'm not that hungry." The truth was, she was beginning to feel a little nauseous from the pain and hoped she wouldn't pass out before she could signal for help.

"Now, honey, check that pack we dropped up there when the trees started to fall. I took an emergency flare and some matches from the saddlebag."

Amanda scrambled up the hill and Beth used the time to drag herself to a more comfortable position. Her left arm was useless, hanging limply at her side. With her right hand she spread the blankets they had used to wrap themselves in, doubling them over and over to form as much of a buffer as possible between her body and the snow.

"Beth, guess what?" Amanda shrieked from the top of the rise.

"What?"

"I can see the town. It's way over there, but I can see it."

Thank you, God. Beth closed her eyes in silent prayer then opened them immediately. There was no time to waste.

"That's wonderful, honey. Bring me the flare and matches so I can show you what to do."

Amanda approached slowly. "You're hurt, aren't you?" she asked and tears brimmed on her lashes.

"A little, but we're going to be fine. Now watch closely. I want you to take the flare to the top of the hill and light it like this. Wait for the wind to be calm before you strike the match. Be very careful and don't burn yourself. Then come back here, okay?"

Amanda swallowed hard and nodded. "I can do that," she said but her voice was a whisper. "Are you going to be okay?"

Beth understood the child's reluctance to leave her.

It was partially rooted in concern and partially rooted in fear. "Tell you what. You go up there and set the flare and I'll sing. That way, you'll know I'm okay."

Amanda giggled. "That's silly."

"I know," Beth grinned. "That's what makes it fun."

"Okay, I'm going. Start singing." She headed up the hill and Beth started to sing.

"Louder," Amanda called.

Beth belted out a show tune and as she concentrated on singing loud enough for Amanda to hear and keeping the little girl in her sights, she realized that she wasn't thinking about her pain. She also realized that she was absolutely certain that someone would find them—they would be rescued and everything would be all right.

Thank you, she whispered.

"Beth? Keep singing," Amanda shouted as she reached the crest of the hill.

Greg was still examining the tracks around Reba when the storm hit and he spotted two people struggling up the hill through the snow. They were quite a distance away, and he knew they would never hear his shouts above the wind and thunder.

He forced Skydancer to travel as far as possible across the new and blowing snow then left the horse and struck out on foot. The snow was well over his ankles and in places had drifted to knee-height. He ran whenever he could, slipping occasionally but scrambling forward on all fours if necessary, all the while calling out to them.

As he slogged through the snow, he saw Beth shelter Amanda with her own body as the two of them hurried around the side of the ridge and disappeared from Greg's view.

"Beth," he shouted. "Stay down."

It was useless. They had not spotted him yet. He concentrated all of his energy on covering the distance between them. *Just give me a chance, God. That's all I'm asking. Let me get there in time. Help me.*

Greg glanced up. He still had half a football field to cover before he reached the base of the hill. He paused to catch his breath and heard the first tree crash to the ground, followed by another...and another...

"Beth! Amanda!" He ran toward the hill, watching in horror as two trees crashed directly on the spot where he had last seen them.

"No-o-o!" he roared and this time his tears flowed unchecked.

The storm passed as suddenly as it had come. The stillness that followed held no comfort for Greg. He plunged on, climbing the ridge, stumbling over the fallen trees as he rushed toward the spot where he had last seen them.

As he rounded the hill, he heard the most beautiful sound this side of a choir of angels. He heard singing. Bad and off-key. And over that he heard the sound of his daughter's laughter.

"Thank you, God," he murmured, then paused and fell to his knees. *"Thank you for saving them and for not giving up on me."*

His radio crackled and he clicked it on. "Dorie?"

"Just spotted a flare, boss," the dispatcher reported then gave the location.

"That's it. I'm here but send the extra help just in case."

"Roger."

Greg clicked off the two-way radio and turned his attention back to the place where he had heard Beth singing. It was quiet now.

He got to his feet and started to run, falling and stumbling in the snow and bumpy terrain. He ran the gauntlet of fallen trees as deftly as he had mastered the obstacle course of old tires that his college football coach had insisted he run every day.

"Amanda!" he cried as he ran and waved to his daughter on top of the hill. "I'm coming. I'm right here."

Amanda waved back. "Daddy! Beth, look. It's Daddy. I told you he would come. I told you." She started running and sliding down the hill.

Greg's heart soared as he spotted Amanda and realized that she was safe and unharmed. Once again Beth had cared for her, put her own life in danger to protect her.

"Beth," he shouted as he searched the hillside for her. When he saw Beth's lifeless body, the fear that gripped him was paralyzing.

Please, he prayed. *Please let her be all right.* He

put one foot in front of the other, forcing himself to move away from his own fears and toward Beth.

"Daddy," Amanda called. "I set off a flare."

"Wonderful, honey. I'll be right there, okay? Just stay right there and watch for someone to come. Dorie is sending help."

"Okay. I hope they come soon. I'm pretty cold."

"It's on the way. They saw your flare, and they're coming," he shouted to her, but his attention was riveted on Beth.

She moved slightly, and he was so relieved that he sprinted the last several yards. She moaned as he moved the tree that had obviously hit her and gently rolled her to her back. "Beth? I'm here. It's going to be all right. Can you hear me? It's going to be all right."

Beth heard and saw everything through the haze of her pain and slipping in and out of consciousness. She found it impossible to believe that Greg had somehow miraculously found them. She figured she must be hallucinating. The one thing she knew was that she had to make sure Amanda was all right. Keep her warm. Get her to safety.

"Amanda," she called and knew that it came out as only a whisper.

"Amanda is safe," Greg's voice told her. An angel no doubt making use of Greg's voice to bring her comfort.

"Blankets." She pushed at the blankets beneath

her wanting to get them free so that Amanda could wrap herself in them.

"I know that you're cold, Beth. Just give me one more minute to check the extent of your injuries. So far we seem to be dealing with a broken collarbone and some nasty bruises. There's a lump on your head. Stay with me, love. Help is on the way."

"They're coming, Dad!"

Beth distinctly heard Amanda's excited voice shouting from someplace above her.

"Good," she murmured.

"Beth says that's great, honey." Greg shouted.

"Did you catch the bad guys?" she managed around the thickness of her tongue and dry mouth. Might as well talk to this apparition.

"Got 'em, ma'am," he replied.

"Good," she murmured and felt herself sinking once again into unconsciousness.

"Stay with me, Beth. Come on. Open those beautiful eyes and look at me."

She concentrated on doing what he asked of her.

"That's it," he said and continued working on her arm and shoulder. "I just need to get this secured until we can get you to proper medical help, okay?"

She tried to nod but her head felt too heavy for any such gymnastics.

Greg. Was it possible?

With her good hand she reached up to touch the face that hovered above hers. The face lined with concern. The face with a day's growth of stubble. The face she had wanted more than anything to see. He wasn't a hallucination. Greg was here. He was in charge. Amanda was safe, and Beth could finally permit herself to slip into the bliss of sleep.

Chapter Fourteen

Beth woke to find herself at home in her own bed. She could hear talking downstairs. She smelled something wonderful cooking on the stove. She was hungry and sore. She glanced down and saw that her left arm had been immobilized. She ached all over and had no idea how long she had slept.

She had vague memories of the arrival of the other rangers. Excited voices shouting orders as she was lifted onto some sort of litter and transported back to the village. She had images of Greg looking worried and voices talking quietly in the background of her semiconsciousness.

There had been a moment when she had opened her eyes and willed them to focus. She had seen Greg sitting by her bed with Reverend Dixon. The minister was talking softly to Greg, and Greg was nodding and listening intently. Then an amazing thing happened.

Greg bowed his head as if in prayer. Reverend Dixon placed his hand on Greg's shoulder and bowed his head as well. His lips moved. Greg's lips moved. That's when Beth had been certain that she was either dreaming or dead. Whatever else might have happened, Greg did not sit with Reverend Dixon and Greg certainly did not pray.

But she was alive, perhaps more alive than she had ever been in her life and she had things to do. She rolled to the side of the bed and attempted to sit up.

"Whoa. That wouldn't be your best move just yet," Connie said as she came through the door with a tray of food.

Beth fell back on the pillows. "I just need to take it a little slower," she said. "Hand me my robe, okay?"

"Not on your life. You're going to stay put for at least a couple of days. Then we'll see about getting up and around."

Beth frowned. "I need to check on Amanda and let Greg know that—"

"Amanda is fine, and Greg knows everything he needs to know. Heaven knows he's spent enough time over here. Now eat a little of this soup I made or my feelings will be hurt."

Beth gave in and ate the soup plus two pieces of homemade bread.

"Well, it's good to see you haven't lost your appetite," Connie teased her.

"Greg must be furious with me," Beth stated aloud the one thought that was uppermost in her mind.

"Greg? Why on earth would he be angry with you? Honey, he blames himself for the wrong turn. He saw that marker weeks ago and meant to straighten it and never got around to it. When they carried you in here last night, all I could get out of him was that all of this was somehow *his* fault."

"Was Amanda hurt?"

"Not a bit. She was cold and tired and hungry, but she was so tickled that she had climbed that hill and set that flare you would have thought that she'd conquered Mount Everest. Greg is letting her think that she's the sole cause of the rescuers finding you."

"She's so brave." Beth's eyes filled with tears. "I really adore that kid. If anything had happened to her, I don't know how I could ever have forgiven myself."

"Here now, none of that. Everything turned out just fine." Connie bustled around the room taking the tray away, straightening the covers and fluffing pillows. "If you're up for some company later, I happen to know a certain chief ranger and his daughter who have been stopping by every half hour to check on you."

Beth caught a glimpse of herself in the dresser mirror. "I can't see them looking like this," she moaned.

"Then let's get you bathed and into something more fetching than those flannels, okay?"

Greg paced the small living room of Beth's duplex. What could be keeping Connie? She had promised that as soon as Beth had had a chance to eat and freshen up a bit, she would call for him. One more minute and he was going upstairs to see for himself that she was really okay. He glanced at the clock on a shelf above the woodstove and willed the seconds to tick by.

"You can go up now, but just keep in mind that she's pretty wiped out yet and needs her rest. Don't go lecturing her because she scared the daylights out of you," Connie instructed as she carried the empty tray to the kitchen.

Greg nodded as he glanced up the stairs and waited for Connie to complete her instructions.

"Well, go on," she urged.

Greg took the stairs two at a time then stopped. He needed to compose himself. After all, just because he had come to a decision about the two of them didn't mean that Beth would understand or even agree. He knocked on the door frame.

"Come in," she said.

She was sitting up in bed, and she looked like an angel. Her blond hair glowed against the dark denim of the sheets. Her beautiful face was scratched but radiant as always. She was wearing a pale-blue nightshirt and he had to resist the urge to gather her into his arms and kiss her.

"How are you feeling?" he asked and thought that there was no way he could possibly have come up with a more geeky opening.

"Much better," she replied. "How's Amanda?"

The atmosphere in the room was laced with polite

small talk with an undercurrent of tension he could have cut with a knife.

"Fine."

"I'm so relieved."

Silence as they stared at each other.

"She can't wait to see you," he said finally. "In the meantime, I'm afraid she's embellished the story quite a bit with her friends. Apparently according to what she told Doug Spinner, she was quite the hero." He smiled and edged a little farther into the small room.

"Oh, but she was a genuine hero," Beth protested. "There was no way I could have set that flare and if she hadn't…"

Tears welled in her eyes making them even larger and more luminous than usual. In two steps he was by her side, sitting next to her on the bed as he held her uninjured hand in both of his.

"Greg, I am so sorry, I—"

"Beth, if there were any way I could take back these last—"

They spoke in unison and then stopped.

"I need to see Amanda," she said. "I need to see for myself that she is indeed safe and uninjured."

"I'll bring her by later, but Beth, you did everything you could. I watched you put your own safety at risk to protect her. How can I ever thank you for that?"

"Oh, Greg, don't you understand that I love Amanda. I know it's impossible to love her as much as you do, but she is so very, very special to me. You should have seen her out there. She was so wise and brave and you would have been so proud.''

He pushed her hair away from her cheek and then ran his hand down her face as if assuring himself that she was indeed all right. ''We've been so very blessed,'' he said softly.

Beth's heart beat in double time. He had said *blessed,* not *lucky* or *fortunate. Blessed.*

''Yes, yes we have,'' she replied. ''It could have been much worse.''

He seemed about to say something but held back. ''You should get some rest.'' He stood. ''I'll come back later and bring Amanda.''

Beth nodded and lay back against the pillows. ''Promise?''

He smiled and bent to kiss her temple. ''Promise.''

She watched him go. There was something different about him, something that went beyond relief that their misadventure had ended well. She couldn't put her finger on it, but there was a marked change in his manner. He seemed… She searched for the right word and found it. *Peaceful.* He seemed at peace with himself for the first time since she'd met him.

Beth smiled. It was a step in the right direction, she thought as she gave in to the effects of the medicine.

''Hi, Beth,'' Amanda said tentatively as she entered the room the following afternoon. She looked a little anxious as she approached the bed.

''Hi, yourself, kiddo. How are you?''

''Fine.'' She was carrying a box that was filled to

the brim. She waited at the foot of the bed. "Are you going to be okay?"

"Absolutely. I'll be back in the classroom by next week."

Amanda studied her closely. "You look okay," she said.

"Amanda, I'm not sick." *This isn't like your mom,* she wanted to assure the little girl. "I hurt my shoulder, and I'll be just fine. Remember when I hurt my back?"

Amanda nodded.

"It's like that."

"Oh." Amanda continued to wait at the foot of the bed.

"What's all this?" Beth indicated the box Amanda carried and patted the side of the bed inviting Amanda to join her. "Come on up here and show me what you've brought."

Amanda set the box on the bed and climbed up, settling herself cross-legged at one end. "These are things about my Mom. Dad wants me to put together a memory book. He thinks you can help me." She grinned. "What I really think is that he's trying to find a way for me to keep you company while you get well."

"It's a good idea—making a memory book—and I can definitely use the company," Beth said. "Show me what you've got."

They spent the next hour spreading out the photographs and mementos that Amanda had collected. As she displayed them for Beth, she told the story behind each item.

"What a fabulous collection, Amanda." Beth fingered the photographs nearest her. It was the first time Lu had been so real to her. "Your mom was very beautiful," she said softly.

"Here's the book Dad got me to put it all together in."

"Very nice," Beth said. "How do you plan to begin?"

Amanda began laying out the items in order, making stacks of photos and other treasures that would correspond to her own life from birth to her mother's death.

Beth looked at each photograph, listened to every story. How could she ever have thought that she might someday fill the void this incredible woman had left behind? No wonder Greg's grief had run so deep. From everything Amanda was telling her, Lu had been a devoted mother—one able to put aside her own illness in her zeal to make certain that her child would one day understand and accept her death.

Beth considered her own role in Amanda's life. What was she to this girl other than someone she enjoyed spending time with? What could have ever given her the idea that Amanda might one day accept her as a part of her life? What had Beth been thinking to imagine that in just a few short months she had the ability to make that deep of an impact on Greg or his daughter?

"Oh, this is a good one," Amanda squealed as she

uncovered a photograph of her parents rolling around on the ground under a sprinkler held by Amanda.

Greg found them deeply engrossed in the memory book project when he stopped by after work. He had heard Amanda's excited voice as soon as he entered the house. She was laughing and he picked up enough words to know which story of her mother she was sharing with Beth.

The memory book had been exactly the right thing. Beth had known when he hadn't that Amanda sometimes struggled with her own memories of Lu. He climbed the stairs, smiling as he heard Amanda relate the story of the day Lu had dragged him into the sprinkler to cool off after he'd come home grousing about some dumb move from Congress.

He stood at the door and observed Beth's blond head almost touching Amanda's dark hair as they pondered some piece of the project. *Mother and child,* he thought.

"And how are the two bravest women in Yellowstone doing today?" he said as he entered the room.

Amanda giggled. "Dad says that I make us sound like some kind of superheroes," she told Beth.

"Well, one of us definitely was," Beth replied. "I don't think I could have made it all the way up that steep hill in the snow and lit that flare."

Amanda grinned. "I had to strike three matches before I got it lit."

"The important thing is that you succeeded,

honey," Greg said. "Help came and that's what we needed."

"It was really just like in the movies when the good guys come to rescue the beautiful lady. When those rangers came charging over that ridge on their horses and there you were in Dad's arms..." She sighed dramatically. "It was so cool."

In Dad's arms. Beth blushed. She remembered that moment, remembered thinking that this was exactly where she belonged.

"Amanda and I have been working on her memory book," she told Greg in an attempt to change the subject.

"So I see. Remember what I said, sport. Save a few pages at the end, okay?"

"Sure, Dad. I'm going downstairs. Mrs. Spinner was making cookies. I'll save a couple for you," she called and then giggled at her own humor.

As soon as she was gone, Greg began putting the photos and other items back in the box. "Connie tells me you'll be getting up tomorrow."

"Finally," Beth said. She felt suddenly shy with him. She tried to remember just how much of a fool she might have made of herself in the past few days.

"Maybe we could go for a drive in a couple of days. If it wouldn't tire you out too much, I thought maybe we could head up to Gardiner for dinner on Saturday." He was focusing on the task at hand.

"I'd like that." *Was this an actual date?*

"Just the two of us, okay?"

"Okay." *No, not a date. He had told her he would*

make it up to her for getting Amanda safely home. This was his way of living up to that promise. "You don't have to do this," she said lightly.

"Nope, I don't. Neither do you, but will you come?"

Once again she was aware of a change in his general mood. "Sure," she replied.

He smiled. "Then it's a date. I'll pick you up at six, okay?"

Had she missed something? He was acting so strange—happy. Maybe it was just relief that this time everything had turned out all right.

"Six is fine," she said. She wondered how she was going to make it through a whole evening with him without Amanda as a buffer to her true feelings.

He picked up the box and bent down to kiss her forehead. "See you then. Don't overdo it on your first day."

"I won't."

He got as far as the door, then turned around and looked back at her. "Good night, Beth."

"Good night."

She heard him go downstairs, heard him whistling as he went. She heard him stop in the kitchen and talk to Connie and Amanda. She heard the three of them laughing. He was genuinely happy and she was downright miserable.

Beth spent the next couple of days helping Amanda work on her memory book after school. At the same time they talked about their ordeal. Beth wanted to be very sure that there would be no residual effects of that experience.

"Dad says that it was God who kept us all safe until he could get there," Amanda reported. "He told me that I must remember that he never would have remembered the sign being wrong or found us so fast if God hadn't taken him by the hand."

"Your father really said that?" Beth's heart beat a little faster.

"Yeah. When we got back here and he was sure the doctor was taking care of you and he thought I was asleep, I heard him call Reverend Dixon. Next day Reverend Dixon came by the house and they talked for a really long time and Dad cried. I never saw him cry except when Mom died."

Beth made no comment but her mind raced. Was it possible that during their ordeal Greg had found his way back to God? If so, then it would all have been worth it. Even her own disappointment that she had made more of the relationship than was possible could be eased by the realization that Greg had found his faith again.

"And *then*," Amanda continued, "yesterday morning he gets up and he's singing and he said something about God being in His heaven and all's right with the world. Weird."

Definitely—but a good sort of weird. Beth found new reason to look forward to the dinner out with Greg. If Greg had found God, Beth wanted to hear all about it.

* * *

On Saturday, she was dressed by five and waiting for Greg to call for her. She had been up since before dawn and busied herself catching up on her school-work and writing thank-you notes to everyone who had brought food or stopped by to check on her during her recuperation. The minutes crawled by. Even a two-hour nap in the early afternoon didn't seem to help.

Finally she heard the door to Greg's unit open and close, then his footsteps on her porch and finally a knock at the door. She forced herself to walk calmly, normally across the room.

"Hi," he said. He was wearing regular clothes and a Cheshire grin. He looked wonderful.

"Hi. I'll get my coat."

He held it for her, placing it gently over her shoulders to cover the sling on her arm. As they left the house, he took hold of her elbow. He touched her as if she were fragile, taking care not to jostle her arm and shoulder.

As they drove he made normal conversation about his day, about the substitute teacher and tales he was hearing from Amanda about how Doug Spinner was putting her to the test. He asked in-depth questions about the doctor's prognosis and plan for Beth's recovery, frowning and nodding as she laid out the regimen of physical therapy the doctor had advised.

At the restaurant, he made suggestions about the menu but let her order on her own. As their food was delivered, he told her funny stories about some of the regulars dining at the restaurant and especially about Gracie, the auto repair shop owner.

Over dessert and coffee, Beth decided to seize the moment. She had rehearsed her part carefully. She would gently introduce the topic of his return to faith and let him take the lead.

"Amanda tells me that you met with Reverend Dixon, that she saw the two of you praying together." *So much for easing into things.*

He looked surprised and then smiled.

"Guilty," he replied as he shoved down another bite of cheesecake.

"So?"

He shrugged.

"You're not going to tell me what happened?"

"I realized that I had been a class-A dope."

"End of story?"

"That pretty much sums it up," he replied. "Are you going to eat the rest of that cheesecake?"

She pushed her half-eaten piece across the table toward him. "Come on, Greg. What really happened? I mean I'm so glad for you—for Amanda. It's wonderful news."

He seemed incapable of suppressing his grin. "It is, isn't it? I mean, when I think of the time I wasted being angry and all bent out of shape because of my own selfish idea that somehow this was about *me*."

"It was about you," Beth said. "That's the point."

His expression grew serious and he pushed the empty dessert plate to one side as he reached across the table and took her hand. "No. It never was. It was about Lu. She was the one in pain. She was the one having to say goodbye to everything and everyone she loved and held dear. She was the one who died."

"And you were the one left behind."

"Yeah, me and Amanda and a gazillion other friends and family members who would have the memory of her to carry with them, the example of her extreme courage to hold up as a model, but who would go on with their own lives."

Beth didn't know how to respond to that. All she could think was that her instincts had been correct. Lu was a saint—a woman whose own strong faith had not only seen her through her darkest hour but everyone she knew and cared for as well.

"When I was out there on that trail, trying to find you and Amanda, I realized that I couldn't do it alone and that made me understand that what I had been trying to do ever since Lu died was do everything alone."

"That's true, but..."

"I was sitting out there trying so hard to find you, to think through how to find you. All around me was nothing but snow—a blank canvas in a way. I was so scared and so frustrated and so angry at myself."

"What happened?"

"I prayed—not anything official, you understand. It was pretty unorthodox when I think of it, but it was there in my subconscious—the need for help, the cry for help."

"Oh, Greg..."

"That's when I remembered the marker and suddenly I knew exactly what had happened. I knew exactly how to find you.''

"That's incredible," Beth whispered and her voice cracked with happiness for him.

"It didn't stop there," he continued. "I was racing Skydancer across the terrain and once again it seemed as if everything were monochromatic—white and more white. Then out of nowhere, there was Reba with her red horse blanket, stamping and snorting like she was trying to signal me. It was like a mirage—just there.''

"But you know you would have found it eventually once you were on the right path."

"Oh, God wasn't done testing me yet." Greg laughed. "I looked up and there you were struggling through those lodgepole pines and I saw the storm coming, saw you take Amanda under your wing as you went around the side of the hill.''

"I never saw you. If only I had seen you coming."

He squeezed her hand. "It wouldn't have helped. I saw the trees start to fall, and then I couldn't see either you or Amanda anymore. I thought God had devised the worst kind of punishment for my arrogance in turning away from him.''

"But God doesn't work that way, Greg," Beth protested.

"No. I discovered that He has quite a sense of humor.''

"How so?" She was intrigued by his story, thrilled by his obvious joy in the telling of it.

"Just when things seemed to be the most bleak, I

heard you singing." He laughed. "It was every bit as awful as that first night although you had chosen something easier than the national anthem this time."

"I beg your pardon. I thought I was at least passable."

"As my grandmother is fond of saying, my dear, you cannot carry a tune in a bucket, and yet it was the most beautiful sound I think I ever heard. Choirs of angels could not have been more magnificent than the sound of your croaking voice."

"You make me sound like a frog," she snapped but she smiled.

"A beautiful frog," he added looking deep into her eyes. "The most beautiful frog this prince has ever met. When I heard that sound, I fell to my knees, thanking God that you were all right. Then I saw Amanda on top of the hill—it was as if my prayers had been answered. I knew then that God had brought you into our lives. I understood for maybe the first time that He had a purpose in doing that. I finally accepted the fact that if I continued to try to fight Him on that, He was just going to keep proving to me over and over again how important you are to us—to me."

Beth fought to control the tears of happiness that filled her eyes. "I am so happy for you, Greg."

"Do you remember telling me that first night you came here that you thought God had had some purpose in mind in sending you?"

Beth nodded. "You didn't believe me," she recalled.

Greg laughed. "Frankly, I thought you were out of your mind. You were exactly what I did not want in my life right then."

And now? Beth held her breath, daring to hope that perhaps things had changed.

Greg's expression sobered. "I'm trying to tell you that I was wrong about so many things, Beth. I have been fighting so hard to stay in control—in what I thought was control." He chuckled. "The truth is, my life has been completely out of control ever since I first learned that Lu wouldn't make it."

So, there it was at last. The admission that losing Lu had devastated him. "She's still with you, you know," Beth said softly. "Just as she is with Amanda. I can see it in the photographs, hear it in the stories Amanda tells about your life in the days before Lu died."

"Lu is gone," Greg said with no anger or distress. "Amanda and I will always carry her in a part of our hearts, but our lives need to move forward. Lu would want that. God wants that."

"It's taken you a long time to get to this place, Greg."

"I couldn't have done it without you."

So, friendship it would be. Someday it would be enough, but tonight it made Beth a little sad—as if something precious had been lost.

"I'll be right back," Greg said releasing her hand and standing. "More coffee?"

Beth nodded and Greg signaled the waiter.

"Wait here," he said as he headed for the door.

Beth was surprised to see Greg leave the restaurant, but he returned a moment later with a large thick book under his arm. When he placed it on the table and removed the protective covering, Beth recognized it as Amanda's memory book.

"Amanda and I wanted you to see this," he said pushing the album toward her.

"She finished it already?"

He nodded and watched as she slowly turned the pages. "She still wants to add a couple of stories, but this is the way she wanted it and you said that it was best for her to decide when it was complete."

Beth nodded as she slowly turned the pages. She recognized the flow of the book, recalled each story. She saw the creativity Amanda had shown in putting it together—the way she had angled and cropped certain photos to tell a story without words.

"Isn't it wonderful?" she said as she studied each page.

She had almost reached the end of the album when she turned a page and saw a picture of herself. And then another. And another.

"Where did these come from?" she asked pleased to see them but mystified at their inclusion in the memory album.

"Amanda took some of them. Connie took those that one day when the kids were playing soccer. These over here are from the open house at the school."

"But why? They belong in a different album, not this one."

"Look closer."

She did and saw that Greg or Amanda or both of them were in most of the pictures with her and if they weren't, Amanda had created a wonderful collage to make sure the three of them were together.

"I don't understand," she said as she turned another page and found only several blank pages completing the album.

"There's a note," he said as he prompted her to look at the inside back cover where he had taped an envelope.

She noticed that his hand shook as he pulled the envelope free and handed it to her.

She slid open the sealed flap and pulled out the single sheet of paper:

Dear Beth,

As you can see, there is still room in this album for more pictures—more memories. I have reason to believe that meeting you was a special blessing brought to me by the grace of God and Lu's loving hand. Amanda and I wondered if there might be any chance that you would be interested in helping us fill up this album—and several more—with the memories of a lifetime together.

Love, Greg

Beth read the note twice to be certain she had read it correctly. Her hesitation unnerved Greg completely.

"Okay, I know it's a corny way to handle this and

after all we've only known each other a few months—although frankly it seems as if I've known you forever or at least wanted to know you forever and Amanda adores you, of course. I mean, the thing of it is—''

''Just ask me,'' Beth whispered praying that the question he would utter was the one she wanted so very much to hear.

He reached across the table and took her uninjured hand in both of his. ''I love you, Beth—more than I thought I could ever love anyone again. You have brought me such peace, such joy, such understanding. You have taken my daughter into your home and your heart and given her the love and nurturing she needed most. Please say that you'll stay. Will you stay and be my wife and Amanda's mother?''

''Yes,'' she replied immediately and saw that he was surprised. ''Yes. Yes. To both questions.''

Chapter Fifteen

Amanda had attended several weddings in her short lifetime. The park was a popular site for such events and as the daughter of the chief ranger she got to watch a lot of them. On the other hand, she had never actually been a part of the wedding party. She wondered what she would wear and dreamed of a white lace gown that reached all the way to the floor and made her look like a princess.

"What do you think they'll be like?" Sara asked, interrupting Amanda's daydream.

Amanda frowned. "Not sure," she replied and sighed heavily.

"My dad says that rich people are different from the rest of us—that's the way he said it—*the rest of us.*"

"Beth isn't different," Amanda said defensively.

"I know, but Dad said—"

"Your dad can be wrong you know."

"Hey, don't get mad at me. I'm just saying—"

"Sorry."

There was a silence as the two of them sat on the floor of Amanda's bedroom stitching on the quilts they were both making for their dolls.

"When are they coming?" Sara asked.

"Tonight."

Sara nodded sympathetically. "They'll be like your grandparents, right?"

"Plus a great-grandma. Beth says I'm going to love her grandmother. She says I'm to call her *Nana.* That's what she calls her."

"That's so cool," Sara sighed. "Just think. You're gonna have all those grandparents plus a bunch of great grandparents and this new great-grandma. That's really so cool."

Amanda's mood brightened slightly. She hadn't thought of it that way, and her real grandparents were coming to town for the wedding as well. If things didn't work out with Beth's parents, it wouldn't be so bad. After the wedding they'd head on back to Chicago and she'd probably only see them about once a year. In the meantime she had her real grandparents and she *knew* they loved her.

"Yeah, it is pretty cool at that," she admitted.

Beth stood at the gate watching the plane taxi into place. She glanced up at Greg who stood stoically at her side. She knew exactly how he felt. A week earlier she had been in his shoes, meeting his family for the first time. She had been unprepared for the sheer numbers of them—parents, grandparents, siblings— some with families of their own, aunts, uncles, cousins. There were even a few members of Lu's family who had maintained close ties and who showed up to meet Beth.

In those first moments of meeting she had seen in their smiling-but-wary expressions that they were as concerned as her own family about what seemed to them to be this sudden decision to marry. But within an hour, she felt as if she had found a wonderful extended family. Greg's mother was a fabulous gourmet cook and promised to share her recipes and secrets with Beth. His father was as gregarious and happy-go-lucky as Greg was quiet and studious.

Greg's sisters were shy at first, but soon fell into an easy pattern of sharing stories of their own wedding adventures and offering Beth advice on how best to handle their brother as well as help with the wedding itself. The most delightful part of all was seeing Amanda with her cousins and realizing what a wonderfully rich reservoir of family she already had to sustain her and with whom she would always be able to share her joys and concerns.

The gatekeeper announced the arrival of the plane from Chicago. Beth took hold of Greg's arm. "Smile," she urged. "They won't bite."

He nodded but there was no change in his expression and he continued to nervously turn his ranger hat in circles as he held it.

"Here they are," Beth said under her breath.

"Mom! Nana! Dad!" She ran to meet them suddenly aware of how long it seemed since she had seen them, of how much her life had changed in only a few short months.

"Where's young Amanda?" Nana wanted to know.

"We left her at home. We thought it might get late and it's a long drive and—"

Greg stepped forward and extended his hand to her father. "Dad, this is Greg Stone."

Her father shook Greg's hand and she could see that the two men were sizing each other up. Then Greg nodded politely to her mother. "Pleased to meet you, ma'am," he said.

"My stars, Beth wasn't kidding around. You are gorgeous," Nana announced.

Greg looked startled and then he grinned and then he laughed and all at once the tense mood was broken and they were all laughing.

"You'll have to excuse my mother, Greg," Elizabeth Baxter told him. "She absolutely never beats around the bush."

"There is no earthly reason to live this many years if you can't say exactly what's on your mind," Nana declared. "I'll bet there's been a time or two when you wished you could sound off to some of those pesky tourists who traipse through that park of yours, don't you, son?"

"Yes, ma'am." Greg replied.

"Let's get the luggage," Beth suggested. "We've got a long drive."

Without her orchestrating a thing Greg fell into step beside her father, politely inquiring about the trip and easily joining in the discussion of the safe topic of sports.

Beth walked arm in arm with her mother and grandmother. "Well?" she asked quietly.

"He's..." her mother began and searched for the right words. "He's not at all what I was expecting."

"He's much better," Nana interrupted. "My heavens, child, you found a keeper with this one."

Beth laughed. "You've been with him for five minutes, Nana."

"I can tell," she insisted. "This one is blue chip all the way."

"I agree," Elizabeth added quietly. "I'm not sure why but I have the most wonderful feeling about this marriage now that I see the two of you together."

Amanda had watched them arrive from her position at the window of her upstairs bedroom. It was hard to really see them well, but it was clear that Beth's dad was almost as tall as her own father and that her mother was the exact same size as Beth except she had this really beautiful snow-white hair that she wore in a really short cut that made her look like a cross between a fairy godmother and Tinker Bell.

But most of all her attention was drawn to Beth's grandmother. There was something about her quick sure movements that attracted Amanda immediately. Then she looked right up at Amanda's window as if she'd known she would be there. She waved and headed straight for the front door carrying a large white box.

"Amanda?" she called in a strong deep voice. "Come see what I've brought you."

Amanda was fascinated. The woman was older than her own grandparents and yet she seemed so full of energy. She bustled around the small living room, taking off her coat and a beautiful scarf she had tied around her neck. Then she kicked off her shoes and settled herself on the couch, legs folded under her as she tapped the large white box. "Open it," she urged.

Amanda approached the box and untied a wide satin ribbon. Inside there was so much tissue paper that she thought she would never get to whatever was beneath it. Then she saw it—a beautiful lace dress, the color of the palest pink rose. Carefully she lifted it out of the box, letting it unfold.

"Do you like it?"

All she could do was nod. *Like it? It was the most beautiful dress she'd ever seen—even on television. It was absolutely amazing.*

"It's really cool," she said softly.

"There's another in case you prefer another color or different style."

Amanda turned her attention back to the box and discovered the second dress. This one was white with a rainbow of narrow pastel ribbons threaded through it at the neckline and hem. It was equally as beautiful as the first.

"Or you could keep them both—wear one for the rehearsal dinner and the other for the ceremony."

"I'll have to check with my dad," Amanda said as she looked back and forth between the two dresses.

"Easily done," the woman replied. "Why don't you run upstairs and put one on, then come back and model it? We'll have a bit of a fashion show."

Amanda smiled. "Thank you," she said shyly. "They are the two most beautiful dresses in the world."

The woman smiled and leaned forward. She held out her arms and Amanda walked straight into them and returned her hug. "They need a beautiful young lady to show them off properly, and I think you're just the right person. Now scoot, before the others come inside. I want you to dazzle them."

With a giggle Amanda took both dresses and ran up the stairs. She was going to like Beth's Nana very much—not because she brought her dresses so much as that she was a really cool lady just like Beth.

"I'll go see what's keeping Nana and Amanda," Beth said even though no one was really listening. Both her parents were spellbound as Greg regaled them with stories of the vastness of the park, showing them maps and explaining the different ecological regions.

Her father was a shrewd judge of character and she knew that he had immediately seen that Greg was an honorable and upstanding man—a man he would trust implicitly. Her mother was clearly taken by his rugged good looks and his gentle demeanor.

Beth smiled as she thought of how he had changed

since the day he had proposed. Gone was the stern manner, the rigid posture and the scowling expression. In rediscovering his faith, Greg had also rediscovered his sense of humor, his ability to view the world as a good place, a place of beauty, and his ability to look upon his fellow human beings with patience and understanding.

"Nana?"

"Oh, Beth, come see," Nana called.

Beth stepped inside Greg's unit and her breath caught. "Oh Amanda, you look like a princess," she whispered.

Nana was standing next to Amanda, a hairbrush in one hand. It was evident that she had just put the finishing touches on Amanda's sleek shining hair by adding a pale pink ribbon that exactly matched the shade of the pink lace dress she was wearing.

"Isn't it the prettiest dress you ever saw?" Amanda asked, reverently fingering the fabric.

"It is that," Beth agreed.

"As Martha Stewart would say, 'It's a good thing,'" Nana agreed standing back to take a long look at Amanda. "What do you think, Amanda dear? This one or shall we try the white one again?"

"I like this one. Is it all right, Beth?"

"It's perfect. I think you may just outshine the bride at this wedding."

"Not likely," Nana said. "Get me that garment bag, dear." She motioned toward a bag Greg had hung on the closet door. "Open it."

"Oh, Nana, it's your wedding gown." Beth choked

with tears as she lifted the beautiful gown from its protective covering. "I love this dress."

"Then do me the honor of wearing it. That is unless you've found something you'd rather wear and have for your own."

Beth could not contain her tears of happiness. "I always dreamed of being married in this dress," she said softly. "Ever since I was a little girl."

"Splendid. Just call me Nana, Inc.—Maker of Dreams Come True."

The three of them had a good laugh and then decided that they would surprise the others at the actual ceremony rather than model the gowns for them beforehand.

Later that night after Greg had gone to his temporary quarters in one of the empty apartments across the compound and her parents and Amanda had gone to bed, Beth stopped by her grandmother's room. Beth was staying in Greg's unit with Amanda so that her parents and grandmother could take over her unit.

"Nana?"

"Come in, child," Nana was in bed. She laid her book aside and patted the covers beside her. "Are you very, very certain about this man?"

"Very, very," Beth assured her.

Nana grinned. "Good."

"I wanted to ask a favor," Beth said.

"Of course."

"Well, since Deanna is due any minute and won't be able to be my matron of honor, I was wondering—

I mean I know it's unorthodox—but would you do me that honor?''

It was the first time in her entire life that she ever recalled seeing her grandmother at a loss for words. Tears filled her pale-blue eyes, and she placed her delicate hand over Beth's. "Your mother will think this is most unusual," she warned.

Beth laughed. "Mother has been dealing with my unseemly actions since I was four. She'll come around. Will you do it?''

"Absolutely. As Amanda likes to say, 'It will be so-o-o cool.'''

They had chosen the Saturday after Thanksgiving for their wedding day, and the long holiday weekend was filled with activity. It seemed as if everyone in the park was involved.

On Wednesday, the children and some of the mothers surprised Beth with a bridal shower.

On Thursday, both families gathered at the ranch where Greg's grandparents lived to celebrate Thanksgiving.

Friday flew by in a flurry of prewedding activity. The park supervisor had given permission for the wedding and reception to be held in the magnificent old lodge at Old Faithful. Connie had taken charge of plans for the dinner following the ceremony and had recruited a team of park residents to assist her. That night members of the wedding party gathered at the lodge for the rehearsal. The informal dinner following the rehearsal was a joyful event in itself as the families shared the childhood and teenaged misadventures of the wedding couple.

Beth found herself pulling back a little, wanting to savor each moment, to observe it and preserve it.

"You're unusually quiet," Greg said as he joined her on the edge of the family circle.

"But not in a bad way," she assured him. "They're all so precious, aren't they? These moments of our lives."

He nodded and put his arm around her, pulling her closer to his side. "Look over there." He pointed to where Amanda and the other children were gathered around Beth's grandmother. Their faces were rapt with wonder as she told them some tale.

"Nana should have been an actress," Beth said with a laugh. "She's certainly a born storyteller."

"Amanda loves her already." He turned her so that they stood face-to-face. "Tomorrow is the day. Any second thoughts?"

"None. You?"

He pretended to consider. "Nope, can't think of a single one."

"Then let's get married."

Greg stood next to the impressive stone fireplace that soared forty feet into the seven stories of lodgepole rafters that formed the lobby of the lodge. His father stood beside him as his best man. He watched as his mother and Beth's mother were both escorted to their seats that were next to each other in the front row. Beth had insisted there be none of the usual foolishness of one side being seating for family and guests of the bride and the other for the groom. "We are fam-i-ly," she had sung dancing around the lobby with Amanda.

The music changed and Beth's beloved Nana started down the aisle. She was dressed in a gown of deep-rose-colored silk and she looked decades younger than her eighty-five years. She winked at Greg as she took her place across from his father.

Next came Amanda. Greg's breath caught. His beloved daughter was dressed in a beautiful gown of pale-pink lace. Gone were her usual jeans and chinos. Her thick-soled shoes had been traded for a delicate pair of slippers. Her hair, usually caught into a haphazard ponytail, fell sleek and shining to her shoulders. She carried a basket of rose petals that she scattered along the aisle as she slowly advanced toward him.

He smiled at Amanda as she took her place next to Nana, then followed everyone's gaze to where Beth walked slowly down the aisle on the arm of her father. A thousand images raced through his mind. Beth singing at the bear. Beth in the fuzzy bear slippers. Beth stealing the soccer ball from under his nose. Beth laughing with Amanda. Beth making dinner in his kitchen. Beth in his arms. Beth. Beth. Beth.

He saw in her eyes that she, too, was remembering the events that had brought them to this moment. That morning he had been up before sunrise and looked out his window to see her sitting on one of the benches that surrounded Old Faithful. She was wrapped in blankets, wearing the funny slippers and warming her hands and face over a steaming cup of coffee. He had stood at the window for a long moment cherishing the idea that he was gazing out at his future. He had never been more certain of anything in his life than he was of his love for this woman and the wonderful life they were about to begin together.

As the geyser erupted with its usual punctuality, Beth lifted her mug of coffee saluting the spray of steaming water. Greg considered the appropriateness of the symbolism—the geyser came and went without fail whether or not anyone was paying attention. Life was like that. These last several months he had permitted it to go on around him, without him. He would not make that mistake again. Beth had shown him the importance of appreciating every moment.

Beth and her father reached the altar. Greg stared at her, unable to believe his good fortune in finding this woman, knowing luck had had nothing to do with it. A far greater power than simple good fortune had brought them together. He smiled at her and received the reward of her glorious smile in return as Reverend Dixon cleared his throat and began the service.

"Well, now, I think it's safe to say that there are at least a dozen people in this room—myself included—who saw from the beginning that this was indeed a match made in heaven."

Everyone chuckled appreciatively.

"Who gives this woman to be married to this man?"

"Her mother and I do," Beth's father replied in a

strong firm voice. Then he kissed Beth's cheek and took his place next to Beth's mother.

"And, in a bit of a twist on the traditional," Reverend Dixon continued, "I am compelled to ask, who gives this man to be married to this woman?"

Amanda set her basket of flower petals down and stepped between Greg and Beth. "I do," she announced as she clasped both their hands and then joined them together.

"Then it shall be done," Reverend Dixon said softly as Amanda stepped back to her place near Nana. Beth and Greg continued to hold hands as they turned to Reverend Dixon and as they began the age-old ritual of exchanging promises and vows, there wasn't a dry eye in the house.

* * * * *

Dear Reader,

Several years ago I made my first trip to Yellowstone National Park. It was late fall and a quiet and wonderful time to be there. Slowly, the park was readying itself for the long winter ahead. The Great Fire had just happened a couple of years earlier—the scene at the end of this book where they run among the falling lodgepole pines actually happened to me!

Our parks are such a national treasure—a gift from the Great Spirit that reminds us more than anything else of how fortunate we are to inhabit this incredible land. One night when I returned to the Yellowstone Hotel after a day spent hiking the beautiful Yellowstone Canyon, I was raving about the magnificence of this particular landmark in a park filled with such wonders. A woman looked up at me and quietly commented, "You've never been to the Grand Canyon, have you?" And she was right—I hadn't. When I did go a few years later, I saw what she meant. It was an equally incredible yet very different reminder of the awesome gifts we have around us that have nothing to do with material wealth and everything to do with being richly blessed.

I hope you enjoy *A Mother for Amanda* and that if you have never taken the time to visit one of our great national parks, you will do so—there's bound to be one near you somewhere. In the meantime, please don't hesitate to write to me. I would love to hear from you as I work on my next tale of Love Inspired.

Blessings!

Anna Schmidt